WEDDING ON THE BEACH

KAY CORRELL

D1530859

ROSE QUARTZ PRESS

Published by Rose Quartz Press

041718r

ISBN: 978-1-944761-13-4

This book is dedicated to my favorite son.
"You are my favorite."
"I know."

KAY'S BOOKS

Find more information on all my books at
kaycorrell.com

COMFORT CROSSING ~ THE SERIES

The Shop on Main - Book One
The Memory Box - Book Two
The Christmas Cottage - A Holiday Novella
(Book 2.5)
The Letter - Book Three
The Christmas Scarf - A Holiday Novella
(Book 3.5)
The Magnolia Cafe - Book Four
The Unexpected Wedding - Book Five

The Wedding in the Grove - (a crossover short story

between series - with Josephine and Paul from The Letter.)

LIGHTHOUSE POINT ~ THE SERIES
Wish Upon a Shell - Book One
Wedding on the Beach - Book Two
Love at the Lighthouse - Book Three
Cottage near the Point - Book Four
Return to the Island - Book Five

INDIGO BAY ~ A multi-author sweet romance series
Sweet Sunrise - Book Three
Sweet Holiday Memories - A short holiday story
Sweet Starlight - Book Nine

Sign up for my newsletter at my website *kaycorrell.com* to make sure you don't miss any new releases or sales.

CHAPTER 1

Cindy Pearson's mother was going to hate the fact the columns supporting the huge front porch of the Belle Island Inn were battered from the sea breezes and in need of a fresh coat of paint. Cindy knew her mother was sure to point it out first thing, and add it to the list of why the resort was such a poor choice for a wedding, a wedding that would take place in just five days.

Cindy sat in her car parked in the curved driveway in front of the inn. It looked exactly like she remembered it from when she'd been there as a child. Well, it seemed a bit older now, and a tad more worn, but charming in its own way.

She slipped out of her current year, black BMW, an engagement present from her fiancé, George.

One thing about George, he sure knew how to surprise her with grand gestures. Her father had been more impressed with the gift than she'd been. Must be a guy thing. Oh, she liked the car. Reliable. It was pretty. But her eyes glazed over when her father and George started talking about torque and horsepower and other car-type things that didn't interest her. To be honest, it had pained her to sell her old Honda sedan that had run faithfully for her for years. She closed the door on her shiny new vehicle, the sun glinting off its freshly waxed surface, and crossed over to the wooden steps leading up to the huge double front doors.

The cool interior of the lobby was a welcome relief from the relentless sunshine outside. She'd forgotten how humid it was down here on Belle Island. Her mother had convinced her to have a tightly gathered, fancy up-do for her wedding so the humidity wouldn't be able to unfurl her unruly curls.

She crossed over to a long reception desk, the cherrywood polished and smooth from years of use. They'd added on since she'd been here so many years ago. Her family had vacationed on the island for many summers when she'd been a young girl. She'd had such glorious times on the island and such fond memories of those endless summer days.

It had seemed like such a logical choice to have a destination wedding here after her parents' first choice of venue, their country club in Lexington, Kentucky, had been booked for all the weekends in June. She was pretty sure her mother thought George would change his mind about the whole wedding thing if they delayed the big day until the first available weekend at the country club. So Cindy had come up with the plan to have the wedding here at Belle Island Inn in Florida.

"May I help you?" A tall, lean man walked out from a room behind the desk. A patient smile crossed his suntanned face. She wasn't completely sure if the smile was genuine or customer service required.

"Yes. I'd like to check in."

"Your name?"

"Cindy Pearson."

The man looked up quickly. "Ah, the bride." He cocked a lazy grin at her then and tapped away at the computer. "Here's the key to your room. The Sunset Suite. Third floor. Corner room. Great view."

She knew all that. She'd handpicked which room she would have, as well as rooms for her parents and the maid of honor, her sister, Vanessa. She'd even picked out George's room. It was down the hall from her, but far enough away that her conservative father wouldn't raise his eyebrow. Most of their other guests were on the lower floors of the resort, especially the groomsmen, in case they got rowdy. Not that she could imagine George with rowdy friends, but so far she'd only met one of the groomsmen. They were all friends from his college days at Notre Dame.

The man behind the counter stared at her. She shifted back and forth on her feet then glanced down at her leather planner she'd opened up on the counter. She looked at the long to-do list and quickly checked off *register at hotel by three o'clock.*

"You don't remember me, do you?"

Cindy looked up and perused the man's features. He looked vaguely familiar in a can't-connect-the-dots way.

"No, I'm sorry. Have we met before?"

"Cinderella Dream Girl."

"Oh." She dropped her fountain pen that was way too expensive to drop. "Jamie."

"In the flesh."

Jamie McFarlane. She hadn't really thought of him in years. She hadn't thought of his nickname for her either, Cinderella Dream Girl. Jamie had always teasingly called her that. All those summers of running the beach, hanging out, and hours spent just talking about everything and nothing. He'd been such a good friend to her. Then sometime in high school it had become more important to stay home and hang out with her Lexington friends than vacation at Belle Island.

"I just... I didn't realize you'd be here at your uncle's resort all these years later."

She tried to keep from staring at his face, seeing remnants of the young boy who had been her friend in the strong-etched features of the man before her. His brown hair still had a hint of red and was cut short. A tiny bit of stubble covered his face in a careless but not messy way. His short-sleeve shirt strained around muscles cut into his tanned arms. She looked down at her planner, embarrassed to think of how long she'd been ogling him.

Jamie cleared his throat. "Do you need some help with your bags?"

"I do. I have so many bags and my wedding dress in the car."

"I can help you with that."

"Still the all-around handy guy here?"

Jamie paused for a moment, gave her a brief nod, and led the way back out into the oppressive heat of the afternoon.

Jamie opened the door to The Sunset Suite and stepped back for Cindy to enter. The midafternoon sunshine flooded the room with light. He smiled at Cindy's excited gasp as she took in the view.

"Oh, Jamie. It's just perfect. The room, the view."

Good. He'd worked hard to get this suite in top shape after he'd learned that his Cinderella Dream Girl was returning to have her wedding at the resort.

His Cinderella Dream Girl?

He turned his attention back to the job at hand and wheeled the luggage cart, stacked high with suitcases and a precisely hung garment bag that he assumed held the wedding dress, into the room. He tilted his head to the left. "Those doors lead to the bedroom." He flipped his thumb to the right. "There's a mini fridge over there by the sofa. Just let me know if you need anything special and I'll do my best to find it."

"Thank you. It all looks great." Cindy crossed the room to the French doors leading to the balcony overlooking the gulf. She tugged on the handle.

It came off in her hand, then clattered to the floor.

"Oh." She turned and looked at him in surprise.

Nice. Great first impression.

He quickly crossed over and scooped up the handle. "Sorry. I thought that had been fixed. I could replace it with new ones, but the old ones seem more in character with the resort. I'll have to work on it again. Try the other set of doors."

Cindy moved to the other set of French doors and tentatively turned the handle. The door swung open easily, and she stepped out onto the balcony. The wind immediately tossed her curls this way and that. He remembered how she used to battle those curls into submission, though he'd always preferred them flying around with reckless abandon. She snatched her hand up to capture her hair into a loose grasp to keep it from whipping her face.

Jamie went out on the balcony and lounged against the door frame. She stood still for a few moments looking up and down the beach.

"I've missed this."

He'd missed this, too. But he wasn't talking about the view. He'd missed her. Their friendship. It all came back to him in a wave of memories. The long walks. The talks. The fact that she'd seemed to get him like no one else. Somewhere along the line he'd forgotten what her friendship had meant to him.

And now she was marrying some George guy, who, he was sure, wouldn't like his fiancée rekindling a friendship with a male from her past. Even if they'd really just been kids back then.

"So, this guy you're marrying…"

"George Middleton."

"How'd you meet him?"

"We actually met at the races. Daddy got a new horse that's doing pretty well for him. He thinks he might make it all the way to the Derby."

That's right, her father was into the horses. How could he have forgotten that detail? Her father could talk endlessly about horses, and Jamie didn't understand half of what the man was saying. It was like a foreign language to him in a world where he definitely didn't belong. He was just the boy who worked at the inn.

He shook his head to clear out the thoughts. "So, is George a horse guy, too?"

"He just enjoys going to the races. He doesn't own any. He's a lawyer."

"A lawyer, huh?" He didn't know what else to say. He wondered if this George was some fancy hot-shot corporate lawyer type. Or maybe he defended rich people and got them off when they really didn't deserve it.

Jamie chastised himself silently. He hadn't even met this George guy and here he was jumping to conclusions.

Cindy looked at him then, with those same honey-brown eyes, the ones that used to crinkle with laughter at some joke he told, or smolder with pent-up resentment when her sister used to tease her about her hair, or her weight, or a myriad of other things. He hadn't thought of Cindy's sister in years. She'd been the most self-centered person he'd ever met.

He couldn't resist asking. "So, your sister. How is she?"

"She's... fine. My maid of honor."

"Really? I didn't think you two got along very well. At least not when we were kids."

"Well, it was expected. Besides, she's kind of miffed that I'm getting married before she is. Well, she's been married before, but she's divorced now. She's been dating again. A handful of the most eligible bachelors in Kentucky, but none of them have gotten serious, much to her dismay. The maid of honor thing was partly my way of apologizing for getting married while she's still on her husband number two hunt."

"Why would you have to apologize?"

"You know Vanessa. She likes to... well... get what she wants. She thinks she has to be married to get rid of her embarrassment over getting divorced. Pearsons don't get divorced. It was probably the first time Vanessa has ever disappointed my parents. Daddy put out the word to his cronies that her husband was the cause, implied in a hushed way that said he wouldn't say anything more. That seemed to smooth over things in their circle."

"And was he the cause?"

"I don't think so. He was a nice enough guy. He couldn't get Vanessa to quit spending and spending though. I know that was one of their problems."

More of those memories of when they were kids were coming back now. How Cindy's mother always nagged at her to sit up straight, speak clearly, do something with her wild hair. How Vanessa would make subtle digs about Cindy's clothes, the way she walked, and her seemingly constant ability to trip over things. He vividly remembered how Vanessa could do no wrong in her mother's eyes.

Cindy walked back into the room and he followed her inside, closing the French door carefully behind him, glad to see the handle stayed attached to the door.

"Anyway, they'll all be here tomorrow. I just wanted to get here early and make sure everything is going as planned. Check on things. You know, make sure things are going to go smoothly." Cindy took a small bag off of the luggage cart.

"I'll do my best to help." He reached for a suitcase. "Here, let me get that."

"Thanks. I'm supposed to meet with your wedding coordinator, Mandy, at six tonight."

"Um, about that." Jamie screwed up his courage. "She's not going to be available."

"What do you mean? She had to reschedule?"

"More like… cancel."

"What?"

He heard the panic in Cindy's voice.

"Mandy's boy got chicken pox, and funny thing…" Jamie swallowed then pasted on a it's-no-big-deal look. "Mandy came down with chicken pox, too."

"What am I going to do?" Cindy tugged at her curls, dashing them away from her face.

"Well… I think you're stuck with me as the coordinator. But don't worry. We've had tons of weddings here. I know how things work." He hoped that little—*okay really big*—exaggeration didn't come back to haunt him. More like a handful or two. But how hard could it be to coordinate a wedding? Seriously, most of the planning was finished. Mandy had given him her notebook. Surely he could just go through her checklist. It would be a piece of cake.

~

"You can't tell me that I have no wedding coordinator. Not five days before the wedding. You can't." Cindy's blood pressure began to rise.

Jamie looked like a boy caught stealing candy. "I, um, I'm sure it will be okay. I can handle things, really."

Cindy was not reassured by his words. Or the look of doubt she could see in his eyes. Waves of memories of their childhood swept over her. The ones where his words were larger than the actual reality. "You're going to make sure everything is set up, the flowers, the chairs? Everything is worked out for the rehearsal dinner and the reception? You're going to run the rehearsal? Coordinate everything the day of the wedding?"

"I, uh…yes. I can do all that. I have the wedding coordinator's notes. It will be fine. I'm sure of it…"

While Cindy knew that millions of people in the world got married without a wedding coordinator, she was pretty sure her mother had never attended a wedding that didn't have one, or quite possibly a coordinator *and* an assistant coordinator.

Do not panic.

"You have no one who can help you?"

"Trust me. It'll be fine. I can do it all. You'll see. Mandy even told me where she keeps the bride emergency box. Safety pins, tissues, hair pin thingies. Stuff like that."

"Oh, that makes me feel so much better..." She didn't even try to hide the sarcasm in her voice.

Panic did take over now. She was going to have to make up a list of everything that needed to be checked and make sure everything went smoothly. She had to make sure the wedding was perfect. And she was going to have to pull off all of that while convincing her mother it was no big deal that they didn't have a wedding coordinator, and that everything was under control.

She swept the room with a glance of apprehension, looking for her planner. There it was, over on the table by the door. First thing, she was going to sit down and make a list of everything she could think of that needed to be checked on. So far it wasn't turning out to be the peaceful, perfect wedding she had imagined.

"We can sit down and go through Mandy's notes, if that will help. And if it makes you feel better, I'm always the one in charge of the food, so don't stress about the rehearsal dinner or the reception."

Cindy let out a long, drawn-out breath. "Okay. Let me get unpacked and I'll come downstairs. We'll go over the coordinator's notes and then see where we are with things."

"I'll put the bags in the bedroom."

She nodded and watched him roll the luggage cart into the adjoining room. This wedding was going to be more work for her than she'd planned. But that was okay. She was going to have the perfect wedding of her dreams.

Jamie left with the luggage cart and a promise to meet her in a couple of hours. She crossed over to the balcony again and stepped outside. The warm sea air washed over her with flashes of memories, reminding her why she'd picked Belle Island Inn for her wedding.

She still could remember all the little details of the day when she was fifteen—her last day on the island. She'd gone out to Lighthouse Point, firmly believing the local legend that wishes come true if you made a wish and threw a shell into the ocean at the point. She'd made her wish for a perfect, fairy-tale wedding, marrying the perfect prince charming. She remembered standing quietly at the edge of the ocean, closing her eyes, making her wish, and throwing her shell as far as she could into the ocean.

Now, all these years later, her wish was coming

true. After months of planning, the day was finally coming. In five days her friends and family would fill the resort, and she and George would get married on the beach at sunset beside the sparkling waters of the gulf. It didn't get much more romantic than that, as far as she was concerned.

The loss of a wedding coordinator was not going to derail her.

Her wedding was going to be special. Very special. And perfect.

CHAPTER 2

J amie was not going to admit he was in over
his head. He wasn't. Somehow he was going
to pull off this wedding. He was.

He sat down and looked at the pages and pages
of Mandy's notebook, all split into neat sections,
checklists of things to be finished, calls to make.
How the heck was he supposed to run a full inn at
the same time he coordinated the wedding? As if to
prove his point, he got called away from his desk at
least a dozen times as he tried to work his way
through Mandy's notes.

If he could make this wedding go off without a
hitch, it might lead to more weddings for the inn,
his goal. He'd do anything and everything to
increase the bottom line of the inn. His mother

deserved at least that, if not more. He sighed and took out a yellow legal pad and started making his own to-do list from Mandy's notebook.

At the sound of a knock at his office door, he looked up to see Cindy standing in front of him looking a bit less panicked than when he'd left her in her room. She'd changed into a sundress and sandals and pulled her hair back into a fancy braid. He remembered those braids so well from their shared childhood summers. She'd always tried to pull her hair back to keep it under control, but wisps and curls always managed to escape.

"Hi." He put down his pen and stood up.

"You ready?" Cindy held her leather planner firmly in her hand.

"I held a table outside on the deck for us. I thought the least I could do is give you dinner while we work."

"That's sounds great."

He led the way out to a table at the end of the outside dining deck and held the chair for Cindy, giving her the seat with the view of the ocean. She sat for a few moments, staring out at the sea, seemingly mesmerized with the playful seagulls diving for their dinner.

"It's so pretty here. I'd forgotten just how beautiful it is."

He turned and looked out at the view. It was beautiful. Most of the time he was too busy to appreciate it. "It is nice here. We should have sunset in about an hour or so. Comes kind of late this time of year."

"Eight twenty-seven."

Jamie laughed.

Cindy smiled. "Yes, I checked. I thought a sunset wedding would be romantic, but it seemed too late for the ceremony."

"Well, that's why we have the nice side area beside the inn set up for weddings and events. The shadow of the inn provides most of the shade, and we've built a large arbor for the wedding party to stand under that still allows a view of the ocean."

"I saw it in the brochure. It looks really nice. When did you add that?"

"Just a couple of years ago. Trying to update the place a bit. Slowly rehabbing all the rooms. The suites are finished now. Still working on the other rooms."

Jamie raised a hand to catch the waitress's attention. A new hire named Alexis, or was it Allison? They'd hired a handful of new workers for the summer season.

The waitress came over and he glanced

surreptitiously at her name tag. Alexis. "Cindy, what would you like to drink?"

"I'll have an Abita Amber beer if you have that."

"A beer drinker, huh?" He turned to Allison, no, *Alexis*. "Two Ambers, please."

"I'm a beer drinker if Mother isn't around. She doesn't think it's a proper drink for a woman. But out here on the beach, it just seems like the best choice." Cindy sighed. "It will probably be my last beer for a long, long, time. George thinks expensive wine or name-brand liquor drinks are the drinks of choice. No use riling either of them."

Jamie sat in silence. He knew Cindy had always tried to please her mother, not that he'd ever actually *seen* Cindy win her mother's approval. But now it appeared it had spilled over to pleasing her fiancé.

"Anyway, you want to get started on the wedding details?" Cindy nodded toward the notebook sitting by his elbow.

"Sure, we'll work for a bit while we have our drinks, then order dinner. Does that sound good?"

"Yes, a good plan." Cindy opened her leather planner and took out a fountain pen.

A fountain pen. Who used those anymore? He watched her neatly write "to-do" across the top of a clean page in her notebook.

Ten minutes into their discussion he knew he was in way over his head, but he smiled and nodded and scribbled down notes. How the heck was he going to pull this off? His mother was off visiting her sister, but maybe he could call her to come back and help him. He hated to do that though, she hadn't taken a vacation in so long and really needed one. He'd figure this out somehow. He had to.

They finished their list making and wedding talk, and he wasn't even sure he'd be able to eat the dinner he'd ordered—not with the knot in his stomach from all his self-doubts.

Cindy attacked her chicken cordon bleu with a relish that seemed to imply she believed him when he said he had this all under control.

He was such a liar.

"The meal was delicious. Thank you." Cindy pushed away from the table and stood up. "I think I'm going to take a short beach walk and try to walk off all the calories."

"Want some company?"

She paused. "You sure you have the time?"

"I do." Jamie waved over their waitress and asked her to put their notebooks inside in his office.

Cindy followed Jamie as he led the way down the steps from the dining deck to the pathway to the beach. They dropped their shoes by the path and headed across the sand. The sun was starting to set and the sky was washed in brilliant oranges. "I'd forgotten how beautiful the sunsets are here."

"This one looks like it's going to be a doozy."

They walked along the water's edge where the calm waves rolled in and over their feet, then rolled back out to sea. The sky's colors deepened with an explosion of purples and yellows peeking through the orange.

Cindy reached down to scoop up a perfect white shell.

"I never did know you to be able to take a beach walk without doing a bit of shelling along the way."

Cindy smiled at Jamie. "No, I don't think I ever have. There's just something about shells. Certain ones call to me to be picked up."

"Did you ever go to the point by the lighthouse and make a wish there? You heard the Lighthouse Point legend didn't you? That if you make a wish at Lighthouse Point and throw a shell into the ocean, your wish will come true."

"How did that all come about, anyway?" Cindy didn't really want to admit what her wish had been all those years ago.

"Well, legend has it that it all started when one of the first settlers to the town lost her sea-faring husband. The woman went to the end of Lighthouse Point and wished for him to return. She carefully threw a shell into the ocean. Months later her husband returned. He'd been rescued by another ship and travelled back to her. So now people think that Lighthouse Point is kind of, I don't know, magical? It's a common occurrence to see people out there tossing their shells into the sea."

"I never knew how the tradition started."

"So, did you ever make a wish?"

"I…" Cindy hesitated. "Yes, I did."

"So what did you wish?" Jamie stood facing her, watching her face.

"Well, it seems kind of silly, and it took a long time to come true, but I wished for the perfect wedding."

Jamie grinned at her. "A Cinderella Dream Girl perfect wedding. I like that. Looks like your wish is coming true."

"Well, except for little details like I have no wedding coordinator." Cindy instantly felt guilty about her remark. Jamie was obviously doing everything in his power to fill in for the

23

coordinator. She was sure he'd do a good job of it... *right?*

A rogue wave rushed into shore and she quickly sidestepped to keep it from splashing her dress. She misstepped and tumbled into Jamie. His strong arms caught her before she fell and made a complete fool of herself.

"You okay?" Jamie held onto her arm, steadying her.

"I'm fine. Nice catch."

Jamie grinned at her. "Couldn't have you plopping into the ocean now, could we?"

"I'm just hoping I can walk down the aisle without tripping on my wedding gown. I swear, I am so clumsy sometimes."

"I'm sure you'll be fine." But the doubt in Jamie's eyes belied his words.

Memories flashed in her mind of prior visits to Belle Island. Jamie catching her as she tripped going up the deck stairs to the inn. Jamie reaching out to steady her as a wave washed over her while they were wading by Lighthouse Point—only that time he'd missed and she'd plunked unceremoniously into the water while fully dressed, including new, dry clean only, ridiculously expensive slacks her mother had bought for her. The time she'd stumbled and fallen against the dining table at the inn and flipped the table and all the food onto the floor, humiliating herself and acquiring a scolding from her mother and a look of disdain from her sister.

"I'm not sure about the being fine part. I have some ridiculously high heels that Vanessa insists I should wear, too. They are cute, but I'm afraid they might be a bit dangerous for me to wear."

"Maybe you should switch to a flat shoe?" Jamie cocked an eyebrow.

"As if I could talk Vanessa into letting me do that." Cindy took one more look at the sun as it slipped below the horizon. "I guess we should head back before it gets too dark." She was having enough trouble walking when there was still light out. Cindy stood up straight and took her hand off Jamie's arm, sure she could walk on her own now without making a fool of herself. *Positively* sure of it...

CHAPTER 3

Cindy sat on a rocking chair on the wide front porch of the inn. Her sister had texted her an hour ago saying she and their mother would arrive any minute. Cindy wasn't really worried about the delay though, it was pretty much standard operating procedure with her mother. Always late. Maybe that was one of the reasons her mother liked George so much. He was always late, too.

Jamie came out on the porch with a tall glass of tea. "Sweet tea? Thought you might want this."

"Thanks. That sounds wonderful."

"I saw you come out here over an hour ago. It's getting kind of hot, you want to come inside?"

"Those big paddle fans on the porch ceiling are moving the air around."

"We had to replace the old ones and get them rewired. These do move a bit more air though." Jamie glanced up at the fans. "It's still awfully muggy out here."

"I'm fine. I'm just waiting for Mother and Vanessa to show." Cindy took a sip of the drink. "Oh, that's good. I swear the inn has the best sweet tea ever."

"You sure you don't want to come in and wait?"

"No, I've just been making notes on things to check." She nodded towards her planner.

"I'm really sorry about the wedding coordinator thing."

"It's not your fault, really. She got chicken pox. It happens. We'll make do." Cindy wanted to reassure Jamie, but she was hoping she was telling the truth.

A fancy red sports car pulled into the drive and Vanessa popped out of the driver's seat and waved. "We're here."

Cindy set down the glass and her planner and walked down the stairs to the car. Her mother slid gracefully out of the low seat and handed Cindy a tote bag. "Here, take this for me." Cindy grabbed the bag and another sack her mother handed her.

"We stopped at a shop on St. Armand's Circle on the way through Sarasota. Bought a pair of shoes." Her mother straightened, not a wrinkle in her clothes from the plane ride or the drive. "I'd forgotten how beastly hot it is down here. Let's go in where it's cooler."

Vanessa looked around, not a strand of her perfectly dyed blonde hair out of place. "No valet parking?"

Cindy nodded over to a lot off to the side. "You can park over there."

"I hope you arranged valet parking for the wedding. We don't want the guests to be parking their own cars." Her mother looked over at the sandy parking lot.

"Yes, that's all taken care of." Cindy made a mental note to make sure it *had* been taken care of.

"What about all of our things?"

Jamie came out to the car. "Here, I'll take them for you."

"Mother, Vanessa, this is Jamie. I don't know if you remember him from when we used to come here."

"Can't say that I do, no." Vanessa handed Jamie an armful of shopping bags.

Jamie juggled the bags and headed inside. He made four trips from the car to the lobby hauling in suitcases and assorted bags. Vanessa rolled her eyes and shook her head in exasperation and drove the car to a parking spot, leaving a trail of this-is-beneath-me-where-is-the-valet in her wake.

Cindy cringed at her sister's attitude then watched while her mother scrutinized the weathered paint on the front porch with a critical eye. Determined not to let their negativity ruin things, she hurried after her mother and entered into the lobby.

"I have your rooms all ready for you." Jamie stood behind the counter now, tapping on the keyboard of the computer and handing her mother a key. It occurred to Cindy at that very instant—how was he going to run the inn and stand in for the wedding coordinator? She fought off a rising panic.

As if her mother could read her mind, she turned to her and asked, "Have you met with the wedding coordinator yet? Everything going smoothly, I hope?"

"About that…" Cindy shifted from foot to foot.

"Don't fidget, Cynthia."

"Well, funny thing. The wedding coordinator came down with the chicken pox."

Vanessa came up behind her. "Well, who is going to coordinate everything?"

"Jamie here has helped with other weddings. He's going to coordinate everything. It's going to be fine."

"I don't think so." Her mother stood tall and snatched some papers from her expensive designer purse. "Our contract says we have a wedding coordinator with our wedding package. And, for that matter, if you look at the brochure it shows a pristinely painted front porch, too." Her mother waved the pamphlet in front of all of them.

"With the hurricane that came through last fall, our building really took a beating. The paint's a little worn, but that's how it is when you live on the ocean. We're scheduled to repaint this winter. Going to wait out this year's hurricane season first."

"That doesn't help us now, does it?" Her mother sent Jamie one of her withering looks that could make a rich CEO quake in his Italian leather shoes.

Jamie stood tall, unaffected by her look.

"Mother, really. I think the place looks charming," Cindy intercepted her mother's wrath.

"Well, we can't have the wedding without a coordinator. Who does that?" Vanessa joined forces with their mother.

"We have everything worked out and under control." Jamie patted the notebook on the counter.

"Mandy left me all her notes, and she's taken care of everything."

Her mother let out a long sigh of disapproval. "I was afraid something like this would happen when you insisted on having the wedding down here in Florida. A destination wedding to Florida. *In June*. My goodness, the guests are going to melt."

"Mother, really, everything is good. It's all under control." Cindy hid her look of desperation by ducking over and picking up one of Vanessa's bags. "How about we go get you two settled into your rooms?"

"You'll bring the rest of our things up, young man?" Her mother barely glanced at Jamie as she turned away.

"Yes, ma'am. Sure will."

Cindy looked up to see Jamie with a courteous smile plastered on his face, but it didn't fool her one bit. He was annoyed.

The morning hadn't gone as well as he'd hoped. Cindy's mother was totally irked with him, and he had to figure out a way to fix it. Jamie knew he was in trouble, but had no idea how to make things right. Master list of to-dos or not, he was only one person. He pulled the inn's battered old van into a parking space on Seaside Boulevard near Flossie's Florist Shop. No one named Flossie had owned the shop in years, but the name prevailed, owner after owner.

He needed to check on the floral order for the wedding, along with picking up an order of fresh flowers for the tables in the dining room. The inn would be full for the next few days with the wedding party and guests, and he wanted to make sure to make a good impression on everyone. They needed some good word-of-mouth referrals. He was determined to make the inn *the* destination for weddings and events in the area.

He slid out of the van and stepped out onto the sidewalk lining the street. Tourists and townspeople alike headed into The Sweet Shoppe. He debated popping in for a piece of pie and a cup of coffee. A quick glance at his watch told him he had about twenty minutes he could spend without getting too far behind, and he really did need something to eat. A piece of pie was as good as anything he could think of to tide him over until dinner.

He headed down the street. The day had already surged to an uncomfortable temperature. Waves of heat shimmered off the pavement of the street. If the heat wave didn't break by Saturday, Cindy was going to have a scorcher of a wedding.

He pushed through the doorway to the bakery and Julie, the owner and one of his mother's closest friends, flipped him a wave from across the room. He waved back and looked around for a table. The tables were filled, but Paul Clark and his wife, Josephine, waved him over to their table. A pretty woman he didn't recognize sat at the table with them.

"Join us." Paul stood up and motioned to the empty chair at their table. "This is Bella, Josephine's niece. She's down visiting for a few days. Bella, this is Jamie. He runs Belle Island Inn."

"Bella, nice to meet you." Jamie slid into the seat beside her.

Julie came up to the table. "What can I get for you?"

"Pie and coffee."

"We have pecan, lemon meringue, chocolate chip, peach, key lime, and coconut cream today."

"Peach sounds great. With a scoop of vanilla ice cream."

Julie set a cup on the table and poured the steamy coffee. "So is your mom having a good time on her vacation? I can't remember the last time Susan took some time off."

"She is. I talked to her last night. She's worried about being gone with this wedding we have this weekend, but this was the time that worked out best for her sister. I assured her I have it all under control."

Julie laughed. "Right. I heard a rumor that Mandy has the chicken pox."

"She does, but don't you dare tell Mom if you talk to her. Mom deserves a break. I'm going to make it work. I will." Jamie could hear the doubt in his voice, not quite covered by his bravado.

"Whatever you say." Julie cocked an eyebrow. "Pie coming up in a sec."

"We're just sitting here enjoying one last cup of coffee." Josephine smiled at him. "I did hear you have a big wedding this weekend at the inn."

"We do."

"Looks like they're going to have a hot one for it." Paul sat with one hand covering Josephine's.

"That's the least of their problems." Jamie took a sip of his coffee. "As Julie said, Mandy, who handles all our wedding stuff, came down with chicken pox. The bride is not too pleased to have me as her wedding coordinator."

"I could help with that." Bella looked at him. "I'm here through next Wednesday, and there's nothing I like more than planning an event."

"I couldn't ask you to do that. I don't want to intrude on your vacation."

"Trust me, Bella loves to organize events. I think she's kind of bored just hanging around with us old people anyway," Josephine assured him.

"Aunt Jo, you and Paul are like the youngest *old people* I've ever met. I'm not bored, but I'd be glad to help you out, Jamie."

"I don't have much budget to pay you…"

"That's okay. I'd love to help. Really."

Jamie was not going to look a gift horse, *er… gift wedding coordinator,* in the mouth. "Thank you. I accept. Gratefully. I do have the wedding coordinator's notebook, but I admit to being a bit lost on most of it."

"How about after this I head over to the inn and look at the notebook and see what all still needs to get done? Maybe I could talk to the bride, too?"

"That sounds great. Really great. I'm sure Cindy, the bride, will be so relieved to hear there is someone coordinating things this weekend. I'm not sure she trusted me to handle it all."

"I planned Aunt Josephine and Paul's wedding."

"And every detail was perfect." Josephine smiled at Paul.

Jamie looked over at the couple. They must be in their late sixties, he'd guess. Very much in love, that fact was obvious from the way they looked at each other. It gave him hope that maybe one day his mother might find someone who loved her like that and treated her like she was the most important thing on earth. His mother deserved that and so much more after putting up with his stepfather for so many years. He was glad she was away from the man now, even if he had left her without a cent. Which was just one more reason he had to pull off this wedding flawlessly and build up business at the inn. He was going to prove to his stepfather—*not his stepfather any longer*—that his mother didn't need anything from the man. They were going to be just fine.

Unless he managed to screw up this wedding.

Mandy had even gotten a reporter from Florida Destination Weddings magazine to come to the wedding and do a write-up on it. If everything went smoothly, it would be a big boon for their business.

He just had to make everything *perfect*.

By late afternoon Jamie had found a quiet corner in the sunroom and Cindy, her mother, and Vanessa sat down to talk to Bella. It was going quite well, if he did say so himself. Bella managed to charm Mrs. Pearson, seduce Vanessa into agreeing with Cindy's choices—twice—and won over Cindy's undying gratitude.

"Now, I have a list of phone calls I'll make this afternoon and in the morning, but it does look like Mandy had almost everything taken care of before she came down with chicken pox. Poor woman, I imagine she's miserable about now." Bella set down her pen and closed the notebook.

"You are such a godsend." Cindy smiled at Bella, looking more relaxed than she'd looked since he'd told her about Mandy not being able to help.

"Well, they did promise a wedding coordinator in our wedding package." Mrs. Pearson was not going to let it slip by that this was the least he could do, to find a coordinator replacement.

"I'll be here before the rehearsal on Friday and we'll do a brief run-through before the rehearsal dinner. In the meantime, call me if you think of anything else or have any questions. I'll work on making sure everything else is all wrapped up tomorrow." Bella stood.

"Thank you, Bella." Cindy jumped up and hugged her. "You are a natural at this, I can tell."

"I enjoy doing this, and I'm glad I can help. I'll check in with you tomorrow." Bella turned and headed to the lobby.

"Well, it was fortuitous that young woman was here to help with the wedding. I can't imagine trying to have a wedding without a coordinator." Mrs. Pearson got up and smoothed an imaginary wrinkle from her dress. "I think I'll go up to my room and freshen up before dinner. Girls, you coming?"

"I'm coming. I need to see if I can do something with my hair in this terrible humidity down here. I'm going to have to rethink my whole idea of what to do with my hair this weekend." Vanessa stood up. "We should make sure the hairdresser comes earlier than planned to do our hair for the wedding. Cindy, call Bella and have her confirm that."

Jamie thought it might be more along the lines of a job for the maid of honor to do, but what did he know about weddings? Even if he had tried to convince Cindy he knew a lot.

"I'll be up in a few minutes. You two go on up." Cindy watched her mother and sister head out the door of the sunroom.

"I think this will work out, don't you?" Jamie wanted Cindy's confirmation, her approval that the wedding was back on track.

"I think Bella is wonderful and I do think it will

be fine now. She even won over Mother, which is a hard task in and of itself."

"So your father and George come in tomorrow?" Jamie was thinking of the reservations. He was pretty sure they were coming tomorrow and the rest of the wedding party on Friday.

"Yes, they'll be here in the morning. Then I think Daddy scheduled a golf game for them in the afternoon."

"Looking forward to meeting the lucky guy."

"George?"

"Yes, he's a lucky guy to be marrying you."

CHAPTER 4

J ulie looked up from clearing off the last of the tables at The Sweet Shoppe. The door swung wide and sunshine poured into the bakery.

"Hey, beautiful." Reed crossed the floor with long strides and swept her into his arms. "I missed you."

Julie heart skipped a beat—a sensation she hoped never quit when she saw the tanned, handsome man. She leaned into his embrace, no longer caring who saw them. He was her safe harbor, where she belonged.

He pressed a kiss against her cheek. "Let me help you finish up."

"You don't have to do that."

"I like helping you here at the bakery."

"I thought you had a business conference call this afternoon." Julie loved that Reed had arranged to work from Belle Island most of the time, even though his job was located back in Seattle where he lived. He'd only been back to Seattle once in the last month. He said he was determined to make doing his job remotely work for him, and prove all her doubts were mistaken.

"I want you to go with me to look at some rental houses. I think it's about time I move out of the inn and find a place of my own. At least until I convince you to set a wedding date." He grinned. "No rush though."

"I just need a bit more time. It is all so... new and different." Julie still couldn't believe she'd fallen so in love with this man so quickly. But she did love him. She just felt like she needed a bit of time to catch her bearings before they actually planned a wedding date. Her friends Tally and Susan said they'd help her with all the details, which was great because what did she know about weddings? Well, how to bake wedding cakes, that much she knew.

She glanced down at the emerald engagement ring on her finger. Reed was being patient about it. He said he'd wait as long as she needed for her to pick a date, though she knew he thought sooner was better than later.

Reed interrupted her thoughts. "I got a list of a couple of houses and two condos that are just going on the rental market. I talked to Harry Moorehouse from Island Property Management. He said he'd give me first dibs on a rental before he put them into the weekly rental pool. I told him I wanted a three month rental, then maybe month by month?" Reed looked at her expectantly.

"I... sure, I don't know how long it will be. It does take time to plan a wedding you know." Well, that's what she'd heard anyway. She had no idea what kind of wedding she wanted. Small, just a few friends, that's all she knew so far.

"First you'll need to pick a date." He winked at her.

"Yes. I'm sorry... I just..."

Reed leaned over and kissed her. "Just teasing. I told you'd I'd wait as long as you needed. I can rent a dozen houses while I wait for you. No problem." He grinned. "Now, let's get your chores finished so we can go see these rental places."

Reed fell in love with the third place they looked at. Well, as much in love as a person could get with a place. The home was right on the beach with a large deck overlooking the ocean. The main area was a great room with the kitchen tucked at one end with a large island. Open, spacious, and lots of windows. The house had four bedrooms, more than he needed. He'd use the master suite, and take one of the smaller bedrooms and make it into his office. The place was furnished in a beachy, comfortable but upscale decor. The kitchen had just been redone with stainless appliances, a nice walk-in pantry, and tiled flooring.

"What do you think?" Reed turned to Julie, who was poking around in the kitchen.

"The kitchen is gorgeous. Just look at this six burner Wolf stove and Sub-Zero fridge. Wonderful. Though, I think you might need some more cooking items."

Reed laughed. "I doubt it. Not with my cooking skills. Unless, of course, you're planning on cooking here. Then we'll outfit it with anything and everything you need."

Julie laughed. "You do try to spoil me at every turn, don't you?"

"I do."

"The place is nice… but don't you think it's a bit… extravagant for your needs? It's so… big. It's pretty pricey."

Reed realized he'd never really talked money

with Julie. She had no idea. Not a clue about what he was worth. The money he'd inherited, and the money he'd made. It was a welcome change from the women in Seattle who had chased after him for his money.

"I can afford it, that's not a problem. I love that it's directly on the beach. And it has a pool. Always wanted a pool. And the pool is private." He reached out for her and pulled her close. "Maybe we could find some time for some skinny dipping."

"Reed!"

"What?" He looked at her with an exaggerated innocent expression. "Haven't you ever been skinny dipping?"

"Can't say that I have."

"Well, we'll have to see if we can correct that obvious omission in your life."

"You're impossible." Julie laughed.

"Harry said the place is ready whenever. I think I'll move in this week. How about Friday about noon? You want to help me move?"

"I have the cake to make for the wedding at the inn, but I'm actually going to bake it really early Saturday morning. So, Friday afternoon will work. We'll get you stocked up on groceries and anything else you need."

"Sounds perfect to me."

"You sure you want to get this one? That small condo we looked at was nice and more economical."

"I'm sure. This one is airy and light, on the beach... and has the private pool." He winked wickedly at her.

She punched his arm playfully. "Okay then. It's your money."

It was his money, and someday he was going to have to explain to her it would be her money, too. And just how much that money was going to be.

CHAPTER 5

J amie walked out of his office and stretched. It had been a long day and his stomach rumbled with hunger. He contemplated grabbing dinner at the inn, but what he was really in the mood for was a grouper sandwich from Magic Cafe. It was a short walk down the beach and the fresh air and exercise sounded like just what he needed. He poked his head into the dining room and saw a smattering of tables filled. Midweek slowdown along with the fact that the entire hotel was sold out this weekend for the wedding, which had put a crimp on weeklong visitors to the inn.

"Dorothy, you all good here?" He walked up to the reception desk.

"All good, boss."

Thank goodness he had a reliable worker like Dorothy. She'd been at the inn for as long as he could remember. Dependable, always had a smile, and knew almost as much about the management of the inn as he and his mother did, if not more.

"I'm going to run down the beach to Magic Cafe."

"Everything's under control here. You go enjoy yourself and your grouper sandwich." Dorothy grinned at him.

"You know me well, don't you?" Jamie grinned.

Jamie wandered outside and kicked off his shoes as he headed down to the beach. A lone figure sat watching the waves. A lone figure with brown curls flying in all directions.

"Hey, Cinderella Dream Girl. What are you doing sitting alone on the beach?"

"Jamie." Cindy looked up at him. "Mother and Vanessa headed into Sarasota for some fancy dinner. I begged off with the excuse of a headache."

"Oh, I'm sorry you aren't feeling well."

"Oh, I'm feeling fine. They were kind of my headache…" Cindy smiled sheepishly. "I just needed a break from them. They can be pretty intense about every little thing."

"Did you eat?"

"Oh, I'll find something."

"Want to go grab something at Magic Cafe? I'm just headed there now. I'm sure Tally would love to see you."

"Oh, Magic Cafe, I'd love to go there. A grouper sandwich and hushpuppies. I've missed that and Miss Tally. Wow, she's still there?"

"Still there." Jamie reached down a hand. "Join me?"

Cindy slipped her hand in his and he helped her to her feet. She brushed off the sand from her shorts and picked up her shoes. "What a great idea. Miss Tally. I can't wait to see her again."

They headed down the beach, with Cindy regaling him with comments Vanessa had made about… well… just about everything.

After about ten minutes they crossed the beach, rinsed off their feet at the spigot at the side of the deck, and climbed up the steps to Magic Cafe.

Tally came walking over to them, menus in hand. "You always come by beach, don't you Jamie?" She smiled at him. "And who is this… wait… Cindy?"

Cindy nodded and Tally wrapped her in one of her signature bear hugs. "I haven't seen you, child, in a month of Sundays. Let me look at you. You're all grown up. How did that happen? It seems like just yesterday you were running the beach with Jamie, here."

"Miss Tally, it is so good to see you. I didn't even realize how much I've missed Belle Island until I came back here."

"What brings you back?"

"I'm getting married at the inn this weekend."

"You don't say. You're the big wedding the town has been talking about for weeks? Jamie, you didn't tell me it's Cindy's wedding."

"Sorry, Tally. I figured my mom would have mentioned it to you." He wondered if his mother even knew that it was his Cinderella Dream Girl's wedding. His mom hadn't been around Belle Island much during the summers he spent here helping his uncle when he was younger.

"Well, I'm sure that Jamie and his mother will do you fine. Susan is a good friend of mine. She and Jamie have done wonderful things with the inn. It's a beautiful place for a wedding."

A look of confusion flashed across Cindy's face, and he knew he'd have to sort things out for her. Before he had a chance to explain, Tally was ushering them to a table near the edge of the deck with nice view of the ocean.

"I'll send your waitress right over."

"Thanks, Miss Tally." Cindy sat down in the chair he held out for her.

He sat down across from her and picked up the menu, not that he needed it. He knew what he was having. He had the same thing every time he came here, except sometimes he had the grouper fried or blackened instead of grilled. Such a man of habit.

"What did Miss Tally mean about you and your mom fixing the inn? So, you're helping your uncle out?"

"No. Ah… he passed away a few years back."

"Oh, I'm so sorry. I remember him as such a kind man. Always had a smile for me. Seemed to be able to do a hundred things at once."

"That he could. Wish I'd inherited more of that gene. I—*we*—my mother and I, own the inn now."

Surprise colored Cindy's eyes. "Why didn't you say something?"

"I don't know, you just assumed I was still helping out." And he wasn't going to admit to her that he sometimes felt like an imposter. What if he failed at running the inn?

"What about Russell?" Cindy's forehead crinkled.

"My stepfather? He's out of the picture now. Divorced my mother a while ago. Mom moved down here to the inn. She didn't have a lot of choices. Russell left her without a dime. She'd signed a prenup with him. She stood by his side for over twenty years, helped him grow his business— you know she was his main account manager when they met and he married her. He finally said he wanted her to quit and needed her as a wife. He liked her to throw parties, entertain countless business contacts, and make sure he never had to deal with anything at home. Then he left her for a twenty-something secretary. I know, classic."

"I'm sorry about all that."

"Don't be. The guy was a jerk. She deserves so much better. Anyway, I was helping my uncle run the inn at the time, so she came to live with us in the cottage next to the inn. My uncle got sick, and she took care of him until he passed away." Jamie looked out at the ocean, not wanting to see pity in Cindy's eyes. "Anyway, Mom's up visiting her sister now. A much needed break for her. Otherwise, I'm sure she could have helped out with the whole wedding coordinator thing."

The waitress came to take their drink order.

"I'll have an Abita Amber, please." Cindy set down her menu.

"Same for me."

"I see you're chancing a beer again tonight." He smiled at Cindy.

"Well, with Mother and Vanessa in Sarasota, I figured I'm safe."

"I could order in a case or so for the wedding, you know."

"Ah, but I could never drink it then, and you'd just make me jealous of everyone who was able to enjoy it."

"You should really be able to drink what you want at your own wedding."

"Sometimes it's just easier to go along with Mother than do my own thing."

"I guess." But Jamie wasn't so sure. He could only imagine the critical cloud Cindy had lived under for so many years. He didn't want to sound disapproving of her choices either, so he decided the best course was to keep his thoughts to himself while they had their meal.

They enjoyed their dinner and left an hour or so later amid hugs from Tally. Cindy promised to come back by before she left. They strolled back up the beach with the golden light of sunset streaming around them.

"I should really get back and sneak upstairs before Mother and Vanessa get back."

"Sneaking upstairs, huh? Just like when you'd break curfew when we were kids?"

Cindy smiled. "Yes, just like that."

They walked in silence, Cindy staring out at the sea as they strolled along at the water's edge.

"Whatcha thinking Dream Girl?" Jamie broke their silence.

"I'm thinking this place is magical. I'm so glad I decided to have my wedding here. I really do think it will be perfect."

"So your wish will come true?"

"Yes, I do think it will. A perfect wedding."

Cindy stood on her balcony watching the moonlight dance across the ocean. Stars were tossed from one side of the sky to the other, lighting the heavens. A lone couple walked along the beach, well-lit in the light from the almost full moon.

She drew in a breath of the fresh, salty air. Belle Island really was one of the most magical places on earth. She had no idea why she'd stayed away so long. The town and its long sandy beaches were like a balm to her, soothing away anything that could possibly bother her.

And Jamie. How could she have forgotten

Jamie? Well, she hadn't exactly forgotten him. Sometimes, when she rued the lack of true friends, she'd tug out her memories of their days spent here on Belle Island. The long walks. The talks about everything and nothing at all. Sharing their dreams. He'd been the one true friend she'd ever had, the one she held every other friend up in comparison, and they all fell short. Her friends in college seemed to be cutthroat and in it for themselves. Her friends in Lexington—and she honestly would call them more life-long acquaintances—were in it for show. It was all about who they knew and where to be seen. She didn't have a single friend she could call up in a crisis, and certainly not one who wouldn't turn and spread the gossip the very next day.

That was a sad state of affairs, she realized it now. She should make more of an effort, shouldn't she? Her bridesmaids were her twin cousins, which she was friendly enough with and saw often, but they weren't friends.

Was the only true friend she'd ever had really just Jamie?

She felt the skin wrinkle between her eyes in a frown. She wasn't liking this poor-little-rich-girl version of herself. Feeling sorry for her lack of friends. Right then and there she promised herself that she'd step out of her shell and make more of an effort to make friends.

There, that made her feel better.

The breeze sent her curls in a riotous mess of ringlets, but she let them dance about her. No one was here to tell her to tame them. They seemed to like to be set free in the night air.

There was something about Belle Island. It made her feel more herself than anywhere else. She remembered that feeling vividly now. How she looked forward in anticipation to their summer-long stays on the island. How she hated to leave each year. She even had a stack of letters from Jamie somewhere. Where were they now?

They'd written back and forth during the school year for years. Then, after she quit coming to the island, the letters had tapered off. She wondered if she was the one who had quit writing…

But here she was, back in Florida, and Jamie was still… Jamie. The one who made her feel good about herself, and always able to draw out a laugh. She'd missed her friend.

She should tell him that. That she was sorry they'd lost touch. That she still cherished the friendship he'd given her. She realized they'd picked up right where they had left off, oh so many years ago with the ability to talk and laugh. He was the one person she could truly be herself with and not be judged.

She turned, walked back inside, and decided to leave the doors open to the balcony while she slept tonight. It might be a bit muggy, but she so loved to hear the ocean. She was lulled to sleep by the sound of the sea and snippets of memories of her summers here as young girl.

CHAPTER 6

The next morning Jamie stood behind the reception desk, talking to Dorothy about their bookings. He looked up when the door swung open and a commotion out of proportion to the two men who entered caught his attention. He recognized Cindy's father. The other man must be the infamous George, the fiancé.

Cindy rushed into the lobby and up to the man with a big smile on her face. George stood a good head taller than Cindy, dressed in what Jamie could only assume were the man's casual clothes—which were nicer than what Jamie claimed for his good clothes. George's hair was cut in a short, precise, this-cost-money style. The man brushed a quick kiss on Cindy's forehead and turned away to speak to her father. Not the reception he thought Cindy would be getting from her fiancé after being apart from him for days and their wedding just the day after tomorrow.

George walked up to the desk. "Do you have someone to handle our bags?"

"I'll be glad to get them for you." Jamie came out from behind the desk.

"In the trunk of the BMW out front." George tossed him the keys.

Jamie reached up and snatched them from the air. George promptly turned his back on him and spoke to Dorothy. "George Middleton."

"Ah, the groom. We have your room all ready for you." Dorothy smiled up at the man.

George nodded curtly.

So far good old George hadn't scored many points in Jamie's book.

George turned to face Jamie. "The bags?"

"I'll deliver them up to your room, sir." Jamie turned and headed out the door, reminding himself the wedding had to go off without a hitch, even if the groom was a jerk. He popped the trunk of the car and hauled in three suitcases and two garment bags. These men didn't travel lightly, that's for sure.

When he'd made the last trip inside, he headed

over to where George, Cindy, and her father stood. "Your keys."

"No valet?" George held out his hand.

"Nope, it's self-park here."

George let out a sigh. "I'll go park the car, then." He turned and headed out the door.

"Dad, this is Jamie. He and his mother own the resort." Cindy turned to her father.

Jamie held out his hand, and Cindy's father hesitated the slightest second before reaching out and shaking his hand. "Nice to meet you, son."

"You've actually met him before, Dad. It's Jamie McFarlane. He helped his uncle with the inn every summer when we used to come here."

Jamie saw the exact moment when the realization of who he was dawned to Cindy's father. "Jamie. Of course."

"Nice to see you again, sir."

Mr. Pearson stood eyeing him, judging him, obviously figuring out where to slot Jamie in his well-categorized world view.

"So, you and your mother help your uncle now?"

"His uncle passed away, Dad." Cindy put her hand on her father's sleeve.

"Sorry to hear that."

Jamie could spot an insincere comment a mile

way. Or at least a comment said just because it was the socially accepted thing to say. He'd forgotten how stuffy Cindy's family could be.

~

Cindy loved her father, she really did, but sometimes he could be such a snob. She sneaked a peek at Jamie to see his reaction to her father's remarks. Jamie's face was masked with a polite, unreadable expression, but it didn't fool her.

"Jamie's made sure everything is ready for the wedding. It's going to be wonderful, Dad. The inn is so charming. The wedding is going to be perfect."

"I'm sure it will, Cynthia." Her father patted her arm. "I'm going to head up and see your mother, let her know we got here." He turned to Jamie. "You'll see to the bags?"

"You bet."

Jamie watched her father walk away and Cindy watched Jamie. "I'm sorry. My father can be a bit of... well, he's set in his ways. Not always the kindest man to people."

"People he doesn't see as an equal you mean." Jamie had a way of pointing out the raw, undeniable truth.

"It's not that..." But, to be honest, Jamie had

pegged it. Her father slotted everyone into a neat little box and treated them accordingly.

"I'm sorry, Dream Girl. Don't mind me. Everything is fine."

George came walking up to them. "Got the car parked. Had to make sure I wasn't parked under a tree. Didn't want to get sap on the car."

George took hold of her arm... in a way that used to make her feel safe, but right now was making her feel like a possession. She shook off the silly thought.

"Come on, Cynthia. Let's head upstairs. I want to unpack before lunch." He dropped her arm, evidently assured she would follow along behind him.

Cindy turned to Jamie. "I made a reservation for an early lunch in the dining room, then Daddy and George are going to play golf."

"We don't usually serve lunch, except for box lunches that most people take to the beach, but I've arranged to have luncheon served in the private dining room while you and your wedding party are here."

"Thank you, Jamie."

Jamie nodded. "I'll make sure it's all set up. Party of five?"

"Yes, that's what I told them."

Jamie turned to load the suitcases on the luggage cart.

"You coming?" George was already headed down the hallway towards the elevator and glanced over his shoulder at Cindy.

"Yes, I'm coming." Cindy smiled at Jamie, hoping to smooth over any hurt feelings her father and George might have caused.

Jamie winked at her. "Everything is fine, Dream Girl."

Jamie stood in the background of the dining room, staying out of the way but keeping an eye on things. Their new server, Alexis—he remembered her name this time—was waiting on Cindy's table. He glanced around the dining room. The flowers had all been arranged on the tables in simple mason jars, but they added a touch of festivity to the room.

"Darlin', why don't you bring us a bottle of Champagne?" George's voice boomed across the room. "What do you say, Henry? Should we celebrate your daughter marrying me with some bubbles?"

"Yes, a splendid idea. Did you get that, hon?

We'll have a bottle of your best." Cindy's father was quick to agree with the groom.

Alexis smiled at the men and hurried off to get their Champagne. She returned with the bottle, iced in a bucket, and placed it beside George with a flourish.

"Why, thank you, darlin'." George reached out and touched Alexis's arm. "Give us just a few minutes before we order, okay?"

Alexis batted her eyes at the man. Jamie had no other words to describe it. He'd have to talk to her. No flirting with the customers, especially ones getting ready to have their wedding here at the inn.

Jamie went back to his office to make some calls, but kept popping back into the dining room to check on the lunch. Secretly though, never obvious, always under the guise of getting something or other. Dorothy grinned at him when he went back for the third time.

"I can't help it. I just want everything to run smoothly this weekend."

"Not judging you, Jamie. Not at all."

He walked past Cindy's table and heard Vanessa and her mother chatting while the men discussed their upcoming golf game.

Vanessa turned to Cindy. "You're not going to eat that roll, are you? Carbs, you're always eating carbs. You do need to fit into your dress this weekend. You should have just ordered a salad."

He watched while Cindy set the fresh baked roll back down on her plate. They were rolls from The Sweet Shoppe and mouthwateringly delicious.

Vanessa turned back to her mother. "Do you think we have time to run into Sarasota this afternoon? Did you see the dress that Cindy brought for the rehearsal? I think we could find her something better than that."

"What dress did you bring, Cynthia?" Mrs. Pearson's forehead creased into a frown.

"A navy sleeveless dress."

"You look terrible in navy, dear, you know that." Mrs. Pearson turned to Vanessa. "You're so right, we'll need to run into the city and find her something more appropriate to wear."

Cindy's face flushed red and she took a sip of her water.

"Hm, what's this? You girls headed into town for a bit of shopping?" George looked at the women.

"Cynthia needs something else to wear tomorrow evening for the rehearsal. Don't worry though, Vanessa and I will help her pick out something suitable."

Jamie gritted his teeth. They were talking about

Cindy like she was some kind of errant schoolgirl. He took a quick glance at her and saw her face was beet red now. He grabbed a bottle of mineral water off the sideboard and crossed to the table. "I thought you might like some mineral water?" He set it down in front of Vanessa.

"Well, yes, that would be nice." Mrs. Pearson turned her attention to the water. "The water here at the restaurant has such a funny taste to it. The mineral water will be nice. Maybe we should order in mineral water for the wedding and reception, too. What do you think?" She looked up at her husband.

"Whatever you decide, dear." Mr. Pearson seemed unconcerned either way.

"Yes, then. Let's have mineral water for the rehearsal and the wedding. You'll take care of that?" Mrs. Pearson sent Jamie a dismissive flip of her hand.

Jamie was glad he'd turned the attention away from Cindy but regretted he done it with the darn bottle of mineral water. Now he had to add finding cases of the stuff for the wedding.

"I don't think we need mineral water, Mother." Cindy interceded. "Plain water is fine."

"Don't be silly, Cynthia. Mineral water it is."

Mrs. Pearson poured herself a glass of the mineral water and smiled. "See, that's so much better."

Jamie got off the phone with their drink distributor. No way they could have the needed cases of mineral water by tomorrow. He was going to have to drive into the city to the warehouse club and pick up the cases himself. Just great.

He stood up and pushed away from his desk, stretching as he stood. He walked over to the window and looked down on the small patio below. It was just outside the kitchen and the staff sometimes took their breaks out there.

As he glanced out the window, he saw George talking to Alexis. She was laughing at something he said. George had one hand resting on her arm as he talked. Maybe George was just talking to her about something regarding the rehearsal dinner or the reception. *Maybe.* That was giving him a big benefit of the doubt, because it really looked like he was hitting on Alexis, and she was loving it.

Jamie really was going to have to talk to the girl. First thing.

So far he really couldn't see what Cindy saw in George, but of course it wasn't his decision to make. He'd never been able to fathom how a sweet, giving person like Cindy could come from a family like hers. He'd never seen her act all snobby or pretentious, and it seemed like she still could never please her mother... or her sister, for that matter.

He understood trying hard to please a person though. He'd worked for years to try and make his stepfather proud of him. It had never happened though. He'd never done enough, been good enough.

He turned when he heard a knock at the door.

"I'm sorry about the mineral water. I'm sure you didn't need something else added to your to-do list." Cindy stood in the doorway.

"It's no problem." He instinctively moved to block the window. "You okay? I see your family still gives you a hard time."

Cindy stepped inside the office. "They don't really mean it."

How could they not mean it? They basically told her she couldn't pick out the dress for her own rehearsal and Vanessa implied that Cindy was fat. She was far from overweight. Cindy had pleasing curves, unlike the stick-thin, almost gaunt look of Vanessa.

"Well, it's your wedding. You should be able to

pick out whatever you want to wear, and serve whatever you want to serve."

"Sometimes it's just easier to let them have their way."

"Whatever you say, Dream Girl. And don't worry about the mineral water. I'll get that taken care of this afternoon."

"Thanks, Jamie." Cindy walked to the doorway, then turned back towards him. "I'm sorry they're all being so rude. I'm sure they don't realize how they sound."

"It's not a problem. Really. I just want things to go smoothly for you."

Cindy flashed a grateful smile and walked out the door.

He quickly glanced out the window and saw that George was still talking to Alexis. Now his hand was covering her hand as he leaned over to whisper something into Alexis's ear.

Jamie spun around and headed out the door, cut through the kitchen and walked out onto the small patio. Alexis jumped up as soon as she saw him.

"Alexis, did you finish up with the after lunch chores? Napkin rolls? Filled salt shakers?"

"I'm just heading in to finish up." Alexis brushed past him and hurried inside.

"George, is there a problem with something for the rehearsal dinner or the reception?"

"I wouldn't know. Left that all up to the girls." George stood up. "I better go meet Henry and head out for our golf game."

"Have a good game."

George walked away and Jamie didn't care a whit if George and Henry had a nice golf game or not. He hadn't been wrong, he'd felt the electricity between George and Alexis. Nice. Two days before the man was supposed to marry Cindy, he was flirting with the waitress.

CHAPTER 7

Bella sat waiting for Jamie to get off the phone. She tapped her pen on the table as she looked at the notebook spread out in front of her and went over the list. She'd made all the phone calls and it seemed like everything was taken care of. She just needed to help orchestrate the rehearsal and wedding and help Jamie make sure things ran smoothly.

Jamie came out of his office and strode over to the small table tucked in the corner of the lobby where Bella was sitting. "Bad news. It was Flossie's floral shop. The order of flowers for the wedding? There was a mix up and red flowers came in, instead of the purple ones Cindy ordered."

"Well, that's not good."

"No, I assume it's not."

"Red is just not going to go with the colors of her wedding." Bella flipped open the notebook to a swatch of light apricot. "This is her color"

"Okay, even I can tell that red goes lousy with that." Jamie reached a hand up and rubbed the muscles in his neck. "The floral shop said they could get a mix of white flowers."

Just then Cindy, Vanessa, and Mrs. Pearson walked into the lobby. Cindy lifted a hand in a wave to Bella and headed over to the table.

"Hi, Bella. Things going okay?"

"We've a bit of a problem." Bella stood up as Vanessa and her mother crossed the room. "There was a mix-up on the flowers. They got red ones in."

"Red?" Mrs. Pearson's eyes opened wide. "We didn't order red flowers."

"Yes, I know. The floral shop admits it's their fault. A new worker put in the order. They said they can provide arrangements of a mix of white flowers."

"We could see if we can fly in the right flowers from back home, couldn't we, Mother?" Vanessa stood beside her mother. "We could try the florist the club uses."

"We don't have to do that." Cindy shook her head. "I think we could use simple white arrangements. We'll use apricot ribbons to tie it all in. It will be fine."

"That's ridiculous, Cynthia. That's not what we ordered." Mrs. Pearson's voice rose.

"I actually like the simple floral arrangements on the tables in the dining room. The ones in the mason jars. Bella, could we do something like that?" Cindy stood her ground… tentatively.

Bella jumped to support Cindy's decision. "I'm sure I could work with the florist shop to do something similar."

"Those arrangements are just too *plain* for your wedding. All wrong." Vanessa shook her head vigorously.

"Well, I like them, and that's what I want to do." Cindy stood firmer this time.

Bella glanced over and saw Jamie hide a quick smile.

"I think you're making the wrong decision." Mrs. Pearson drew herself up to her full height and set her shoulders firmly. "But then, you wanted the wedding down here in this unbearably humid little town, when your father and I would have given you the perfect wedding anywhere in the country."

"This *is* the perfect place, Mother." Cindy's voice was low but full of conviction.

Mrs. Pearson let out a long sigh. "Fine. If you

want some ridiculous arrangement in *jars*, for goodness sakes, then it's on your head when people are talking about it."

"But, Mother. It's so embarrassing. She can't do that." Vanessa practically stamped her feet in disagreement.

"But I *am* doing that, Vanessa. And they'll look lovely." Cindy turned and walked out the door of the lobby.

Jamie thought it would probably be rude of him to give a standing ovation or a slow clap for Cindy as she walked out of the lobby. Good for her. She'd finally stood up to her mother and Vanessa.

"Mother, we can't let her do that." Vanessa stood there brimming with ire.

Mrs. Pearson turned to Bella. "Make sure those floral arrangements don't embarrass me. *Do* something with them."

Bella wrote a note in the notebook and watched Vanessa and Mrs. Pearson leave the lobby.

"Well, that was interesting." Bella turned to Jamie.

"Yes, it was. First time I've seen Cindy stand up to them. To be honest, simple arrangements do seem more Cindy's style. I think this whole wedding has just been Vanessa forcing her opinions on Cindy."

"Weddings can be stressful times for families." Bella set her pen on the table. "So, any more bad news?"

"I'm hoping that's about the end of it. I'm really grateful for you doing all this. I can't thank you enough. There's a free vacation week for you at the inn if you want it. Just to show how much I really do truly appreciate you."

"Might take you up on that with my two best friends from back home. We keep saying we're going to have a girls' getaway."

"That would be great. Anytime." Jamie felt relief wash over him with the flower situation handled. "I need to run into the city to get mineral water. Mrs. Pearson has decided she wants to serve that instead of our regular water. Got to head to the warehouse store for it. Do you need me to pick up anything while I'm there?"

"I think we have everything else all sorted out."

"You're a lifesaver."

Bella grinned at him. "I'm a planner. And very organized. Well, organized about stuff like this and my business. Not so much my house and home life."

"Well, if you ever want to move here and become an event planner, you just let me know."

"Pretty sure that will never happen, but I sure do love coming here to visit Aunt Jo."

"The timing of your trip this time was sure lucky for me."

"Well, let's see if we can hold onto that luck a bit longer, and try not to let anything else go wrong."

"From your lips to the wedding angels' ears."

Cindy was pretty sure she'd tried on two dozen dresses in an hour's time. She walked out of the dressing room to where her mother and Vanessa sat on satin tufted settees and sipped on glasses of Champagne.

"That one makes you look skinnier than you are." Vanessa held up her glass in an attempt to point.

"The color makes her look a bit washed out though." Her mother cocked her head and looked critically at her. "But it might be the best of the bunch. Try on those last few dresses, Cynthia."

Cindy gritted her teeth and walked silently back into the dressing room. She looked at the dresses scattered around the dressing room, mocking her. How had she let this turn into a dress-the-Cindy-doll session?

The boutique worker came in with a handful of dresses and a look of apology on her face. "Here are a few more in your size." The woman hung them on a rack in the dressing area.

Cindy walked over to the newly delivered garments and sifted through them. A simple off-white dress with a bit of lavender trim caught her eye. While her mother and Vanessa had her trying on shift cut dresses, this one was fitted at the top with a loose, flowy skirt. She loved it at first sight.

She took it off the hanger and slipped it on. It fit like it had been handmade for her. This was the dress. The one. She straightened her shoulders and walked out to face her mother and Vanessa.

"Really, Cynthia? That's not what we discussed. We agreed on simple and elegant. A simple slim cut." Her mother shook her head.

Vanessa raised an eyebrow and grimaced.

"Well, I love this dress. This is the one I'm going to wear. The ones you picked out for me are just not... well, they aren't me. This one is and it's lovely."

"It does hide your hips." Vanessa tossed the comment like it was a compliment.

"But it certainly isn't elegant. It's just so... casual." Her mother eyed her critically. "I guess we could dress it up with jewelry and some nice heels."

"I'm wearing flats. I have some off-white ones that will look great with this." Cindy stood her ground. *Kind of.* She was still afraid they'd talk her out of the dress.

"Well, I'm tired of watching her parade around in dresses anyway. Wear that one if you want. We at least tried to get you to buy an appropriate dress." Vanessa took the last sip of her Champagne and rose from the settee with practiced grace.

Her mother stood, set down her glass, and turned to the boutique worker. "I guess we'll take that one."

Cindy was pretty sure her mother's long-suffering, tired sigh was heard throughout the store.

"Go change and we'll head back to the inn. I want to lie down for a bit before dinner." Her mother turned and walked away.

Cindy headed back into the dressing room and slipped out of the dress. She liked it better than the navy slip dress she had originally brought to wear in an attempt to please her mother. She was pretty sure her mother wished she'd never brought up the shopping trip.

With a little smile, Cindy hung up the dress

and slipped into her clothes. The worker came and whisked the dress away. Cindy took one last look in the mirror, surprised to see there was still the hint of a smile on her face. It felt good to stand up to Vanessa and her mother. Really good.

Cindy lingered behind her mother and sister as they headed into the lobby of the inn. They were headed up to rest before dinner, but she was strangely wound up after the big dress buying expedition. She pushed through the door of the inn, wrestling with the dress hanging in a garment bag. The cool air wrapped around her, a welcome relief from the late afternoon humidity.

"Hey, Dream Girl, looks like you found your dress for the ball." Jamie stood behind the counter with a lazy grin across his face.

She crossed the lobby and draped the dress across the counter. "I did. It's perfect, though Mother and Vanessa disagree with me."

"I thought the whole point was they wanted to pick one out for you…"

"Well, let's just say we couldn't agree on one. So I went with one I love."

A look of approval flashed across Jamie's face.

"Well, good for you. I'm sure you'll look beautiful."

"Thanks, Jamie." She felt the heat of a blush drift across her cheeks. That was the kindest thing anyone had said to her today, even if he was just saying it to be nice.

"So what are your plans for tonight?"

"We're meeting down at the outside bar here for your happy hour, then we're headed out for dinner at Magic Cafe. I'm not sure that's exactly the kind of place that George likes to eat. He usually prefers the fancy linen tablecloth restaurants with good wine lists, but my father likes the fish there, so Miss Tally is going to hold the big table in the corner for us. At least I'm sure he'll be impressed with the view."

"I guess I'll see you down here later, then. I'm the bartender for happy hour tonight."

"You're just a jack of all trades around here now, aren't you?"

"More of a Jamie of all trades." He winked at her.

Cindy laughed out loud, the first time in hours that she'd felt relaxed. Honestly, she hadn't felt this relaxed since she and Jamie had eaten at Magic Cafe. Though it was possible a bride wasn't supposed to get to relax at all during her wedding week.

CHAPTER 8

J amie set up the bar area for their nightly
happy hour. They'd put in a Tiki-style bar at
one side of their huge decked area. There were
stools at the bar, and scattered tables and
Adirondack chairs around the area. A bit of a breeze
had picked up from the ocean and blown away the
oppressive humidity of earlier today. It was really
nice evening weather and Jamie was expecting to be
busy during the two-hour happy hour. He looked
over at the beach and saw that many people had
called it a day. The beach workers were closing up
umbrellas and putting them in the large wooden
boxes for the evening. The waves had kicked up a
bit, rolling up onto the beach in contrast to the
almost lake-like calm of earlier today. He loved this

time of day. From early evening until sunset seemed like the perfect time on the southern Gulf Coast of Florida.

Alexis came walking over with another tray of glasses. "Here you go." She set the tray on the counter and he picked it up and swung it under the counter. When the waitresses worked happy hour they were allowed to wear shorts and a Belle Island Inn t-shirt. Alexis has taken that to heart with short shorts and a tight t-shirt. Maybe he'd have to revise their dress code for happy hour workers…

He glanced up and saw George stop Alexis as she headed back inside for another tray of glasses. George rested his hand on Alexis's shoulder and she tossed her blonde hair while reaching a hand up to brush George's. George slipped his hand down to the small of Alexis's back and leaned over to say something to her. He could see her nod. *She'd better be agreeing to bring the guy a drink and nothing more.*

George sauntered over to the bar and slipped onto a bar stool. "I'm a bit early, but that doesn't matter does it? I'll have a bourbon. Your best. Neat."

Jamie noticed that George didn't wait for an answer. Well, there goes his theory that Alexis was agreeing to bring George a drink.

Jamie poured the man a drink, hoping he'd just

get up and go walk over to the Adirondack chairs with the view of the ocean. No such luck. The man sat and sipped his bourbon at the bar.

"So, Cynthia tells me your family owns the inn."

"We do."

"I hope you can handle all the guests we have coming for the wedding."

"I'm sure we can." Jamie slammed down the bucket of ice a bit harder than needed, and busied himself slicing up a lime. He'd better be careful or he was going to cut off his finger.

"Cynthia assures me you have everything under control. I hope so. I have some important business contacts coming to the wedding. They are staying in Sarasota, of course. I found a couple of luxury resorts to recommend to them."

Jamie wasn't sure if the man was clueless at how rude he was, or possibly baiting him to see a reaction. Either way, he wasn't impressed with this George guy. He must have some redeeming qualities though, otherwise, what the heck was Cindy doing with him?

Jamie reached for a lemon to slice. "Yes, we didn't have room here at the inn for everyone coming to the wedding. There are a handful of other nice places to stay on Belle Island though."

George looked at him and cocked an eyebrow in what could only be considered disbelief. "I know Cynthia has some kind of silly romantic notion this place will be perfect for her wedding. We couldn't get the club for the wedding, so I let her choose wherever she wanted. I hope it all works out. It's a bit more… rustic… than I'd imagined."

Okay, at this point Jamie admitted he just did not like the man.

At all.

Alexis walked up with a second tray of glasses. She seemed to think the only open spot at the bar was right next to George and stood inches away from him and passed the tray over to Jamie.

George swirled the bourbon in his glass and grinned at Alexis. "Will you be a darlin' and bring us our drinks if I move over to that table over there and wait for everyone to show up?"

Alexis slipped on a suggestive smile and nodded. "I sure will. Here, let's get you all settled."

George stood up and followed behind Alexis, staring at her short shorts. Or more likely, the long, tanned legs sticking out of the short shorts.

Cindy walked out into the early evening sunshine.

She squinted her eyes against the brightness, plucked her sunglasses from their perch atop her head, and slid them onto her face. Better. Much better. She looked around and saw George across the way, talking to the waitress. The girl bent over George, hovering close, to hand him a drink. Cindy was pretty sure if the girl's shorts were any shorter they wouldn't leave much to anyone's imagination. The girl stood, threw back her head and laughed at something George had said to her. George reached out and touched her arm as the girl stood talking to him.

Laughing.

Hanging on George's every word.

Cindy heard Jamie's voice tossed around on the gentle sea breeze. "Alexis, we need more glasses."

The girl turned toward the Tiki hut where Jamie stood, then reluctantly pulled away from George. As the girl walked away, Cindy saw George watching the girl's backside. That was one thing that had taken Cindy a long time to get used to. George's eye for a pretty girl. Their front, their back, their legs. Whatever caught his eye. In her fantasy, she thought a man fell in love with a woman and never had a roving eye for anyone else. George shot that theory down. *Completely*. It still annoyed her that George was so obvious about it though. When she'd mentioned it to Vanessa, her sister had laughed at her and told her to grow up, that all men were like that.

Cindy slid on a smile with an it's-not-going-to-bug-me-now shrug and walked over to where Jamie was serving drinks.

"Hey, Dream Girl. What can I get you?"

Cindy took a quick look over at George, wanting to order a beer in retaliation for George's wandering eye, but knowing her mother would show up any moment and give her the evil eye if she had a beer in her hand. "Pinot grigio."

"You got it." Jamie smiled at her. He poured the wine and handed it to her. "Your George fella is over there." Jamie nodded his head towards the sitting area across the way.

"Thanks. Yes, I saw him. Headed that way now." Cindy turned, walked across the deck and settled into the chair beside George. He leaned over, gave her a perfunctory kiss on the cheek, and went back to sipping his drink. The place on her face where he'd pressed the quick kiss tingled with…*with what?* Wanting more? Wishing he actually missed her when they were apart and showed her just how much?

She looked down at her wine glass—that she really wished was an ice cold beer mug—and then back at George. He was watching a group of twenty-something women in impossibly tiny bikinis as they came up from the beach and crossed over to the Tiki hut. He nodded almost imperceptibly in appreciation of the view.

She realized with a start that she'd never once seen him look at her with that kind of appreciation. Like she was pretty or special or…

She put her wine glass down on the table between her and George. "I'll be right back." She pushed out of the chair and crossed over to the bar.

Jamie finished up serving the group of women and they headed off to lounge on some chairs on the deck. He looked up to see Cindy standing before him.

"Everything okay?" He'd just served her a few minutes before. He glanced over to where George was sitting—watching the bikini-clad girls—and saw Cindy's wine glass sitting on the table beside him.

"I'll have that beer." Cindy slipped onto a barstool.

"You will?" Jamie nodded in approval and drew her a cold beer from the tap. "Here you go. Enjoy."

"I will." Cindy's voice held an edge of defiance.

Jamie watched her spin off the bar stool and cross the distance over to George. Her dress blew and swirled around her in the breeze. She looked like a vision of a determined whirlwind as she crossed the distance.

Jamie pulled his stare from Cindy to George to see the man's reaction. No man could be immune to the view of Cindy crossing that deck. She looked… beautiful. Spectacular.

But all the man did was scowl when he saw the beer in Cindy's hand. She dropped into her seat and took a sip of it, either not seeing or ignoring the obvious disapproval of her fiancé.

Cindy's parents and sister walked up to the bar, and Jamie pulled his attention away from Cindy.

"You'll send someone over to get our drink order. We'll be over by Cynthia and George." Cindy's mom didn't so much ask a question, as make a demand.

"Sure will." Jamie nodded. Most people just came up to the bar and ordered at their informal happy hour, so Alexis was the only waitress on bar duty tonight. He wasn't thrilled about sending her back over to George.

Jamie saw Cindy's mom send her a disapproving

glare when Cindy took a drink of her beer. Jamie couldn't help but smile.

He reluctantly sent Alexis over to get their drink orders, but to her credit, she didn't flirt—much—with Cindy and all her family sitting right next to George.

He pulled his attention to another group headed to the bar. Paul, Josephine, and Bella walked up.

"Jamie, lad. We decided to come have dinner here at the inn, but thought a drink on the deck beforehand was in order." Paul helped Josephine onto a barstool. "Bella wanted to check on something or other about the wedding, too."

"Everything okay?" Jamie looked at Bella.

"Yes, everything is fine. Don't worry so much. It's going to be the wedding beyond compare, trust me." Bella smiled and slipped onto a barstool. The trio sat and chatted with him about Belle Island news while they enjoyed their drinks.

He noticed Cindy and her family get up from their seats and head inside. Cindy stopped by the bar on her way in.

"Bella, I'll see you at ten in the morning? We'll go over everything again?" Cindy stood by Bella's seat.

"Yes. Don't worry about a thing. Everything is all going as planned."

"I really appreciate your help." Cindy turned, gave them all a quick wave, and headed after her family.

Bella nodded toward the departing group. "So, everything's going okay with them? Cindy's mom get all settled down? I tried my best to assuage her fears."

"I think so. I mean, I don't know." Jamie sighed. "I just need this wedding to be pulled off without a hitch. I'm banking on getting some good word of mouth for using the inn as a destination wedding spot."

"I'm doing everything I can." Bella set down her drink. "I think it will all go fine."

"I'm sure it will, dear." Josephine patted Bella's hand. "You know how good you are with making sure events go smoothly."

"To be honest, I'm a bit worried about the bride and groom." Bella leaned on the bar.

Jamie cocked his head, listening intently.

"The groom just seems... well... not how I expect a groom to act. I might be a hopeless romantic, but I expect a groom to act like he's such a lucky guy to be marrying his bride. To act like... well, like he's in love with her. Besotted, even. But I swear he acts like he's closing a business deal with Cindy's father." Bella shook her head. "Oh, I shouldn't have said that. I don't really know them."

Jamie had to bite his tongue. What he wanted to say was that George was a jerk and didn't appreciate the fabulous woman who had said yes to his proposal of marriage. And while he was at it he'd like to add in that Cindy's family didn't appreciate her either. But he stayed silent.

"Some people just don't show their emotions well." Paul entered the conversation.

"Well, you certainly let everyone know that you're nuts about my aunt." Bella grinned.

Paul leaned over and placed a quick kiss on Josephine's forehead. "I am crazy about this woman. I'm the luckiest guy in the world."

"And that is the kind of love I wish Cindy had found." Jamie just couldn't help himself. He had to say it.

"That's the kind of love that makes a marriage strong and brings joy and happiness to the couple." Bella paused and took a sip of her drink. "Maybe he's just the reserved kind of guy."

"Maybe." Jamie wiped the bar in front of him, unduly sad about Cindy possibly headed into a marriage that… well, it didn't appear it would be full of the love and appreciation she deserved.

CHAPTER 9

Cindy smiled as she and her family pulled up to Magic Cafe. She loved the place and hoped that George would find it as charming as she did. If she'd had her way, they would have strolled here on the beach, but her family and George had vigorously vetoed that idea.

The restaurant was in an old shingled building with a mismatch of additions constructed over the years, which somehow gave it charm, not disarray. A long porch stretched across the front, with rocking chairs and benches for the crowded times when people had to wait for their tables.

They all got out of the car and crossed the sandy parking lot to the entrance to the restaurant. "This town isn't much on valet parking, is it?" George reached down and dusted the sand from his leather loafers as he stepped up on the porch in front of the cafe.

Cindy chose to ignore the remark. There was ample parking in the lot and they hadn't been twenty steps from the door.

George was a bit of a snob.

Cindy froze in her tracks. Had she just thought that? Really? Maybe the thought had always been there, way in the back of her mind, but she hadn't ever really *thought* it. She eyed him critically as he dusted off the other shoe. She'd been so focused on how well he fit in with her family. How he wanted to marry her. *Her.* With her ability to stumble and lack of style with her clothing. With her flyaway hopeless curls and awkwardness at parties. He was gallant and charming, with a sense of humor. Though, if she were honest, the humor was sometimes targeted towards others and it made her feel a bit uncomfortable.

Just then George turned toward her and flashed his ever-so-disarming smile and held out his hand. "Coming, sweetheart?"

She took his hand, and all of her uncharitable thoughts just vanished as quickly as they'd swept over her. She was just being a silly, nervous bride.

Miss Tally ushered them to a large table outside

near the beach. A wonderful breeze kept the humidity at bay and the temperature was perfect for an outside dinner.

"We should have asked for a table inside in the air conditioning." Vanessa looked up at the paddle fans lazily spinning in the ceiling above them.

"I love eating outside here. We'll get the fabulous view of the sunset." Cindy was not letting her sister's negativity ruin her evening.

George squeezed her hand then held out her chair. "This is just fine. If this is what my bride-to-be wants, this is what she gets."

Cindy slipped into the chair and smiled up at him gratefully for taking her side.

Cindy's parents sat and her father turned to the waitress. "George and I will both have a glass of your finest bourbon, right George?"

"Right, Henry."

"What brands do you have, hon?" Her father looked at the waitress.

The waitress listed off their top-shelf brands and her father was not impressed. He ordered their drinks with a sigh.

"That will just have to make do for us, old boy." Her father shook his head and looked at George.

"Sure. That will work." George looked just

slightly annoyed, as if the brand of bourbon was going to ruin their meal.

"What would you ladies like?" The waitress turned to the women.

Her mother and sister picked up the drink menu and looked at the wines on one side and beer list on the back. The menu was a simple cardboard, covered in vinyl. Vanessa kept turning it over and over. "Well, I'll have a glass of your best cabernet."

"I'll have the same." Her mother set down the drink menu and wiped her hands on her napkin.

"I'll have a beer." Cindy couldn't help herself.

"Cynthia, I don't know what has come over you. I certainly hope you don't plan on ordering a beer tomorrow at the rehearsal, or having one at the wedding." Her mother looked appalled.

"There are a lot of calories in beer." Vanessa gave her sister a pointed stare.

The waitress looked at her, waiting to see if she would change her order.

"The Abita beer please."

Her mother shook her head.

They ordered their meals, and George and her father talked cars while they waited for dinner. Endlessly about cars. Vanessa and her mother talked shoes. Endlessly about shoes.

Cindy sat quietly between the two conversations

and a wave of loneliness swept over her. She was sitting between her fiancé—the man she was marrying in two days and spending the rest of her life with—and her family, yet she was lonelier than she'd ever felt. An outsider at a dinner that was to celebrate her upcoming wedding. Her heart plummeted and she looked around in a bit of a panic.

It's just wedding nerves. That's all.

The waitress brought their meals. Her mother sent hers back saying the steak wasn't cooked correctly, even though it looked like a perfect medium to Cindy. Who orders steak anyway when the restaurant was known for its fish?

Vanessa pushed around the fries and hushpuppies on her plate saying there was just too much fried food with her dinner.

Cindy ate her grouper—fried—and every bite of her hushpuppies.

"If we ever come here again," George said in a loud voice, "we'll have to bring our own bourbon."

"Well, I can't imagine why we'd be here again, but if we ever are, we'll bring some good wine, too." Vanessa's voice rang out over the strangely quiet restaurant.

Cindy was aware that the locals were staring at them in an unfriendly way. She couldn't blame them. No one criticizes Miss Tally or her cafe. The town loved her. Cindy loved her. She couldn't help but take her family's snobbish criticism to heart.

"Well, I think this was the best grouper I've ever had. How often do you get wonderful food like this, and this view? Look at that beautiful sunset. All the oranges and purples and yellows." Cindy swept an arm in the direction of the sunset.

"Henry, how about we head back and have a cigar at the inn. I saw an outside fire pit near the beach. We could have it there. I've stashed some good bourbon in the room. We'll grab it." George pushed back his chair.

It was like her family ignored her. No, it wasn't *like* her family ignored her. They *did* ignore her. She was invisible. That annoying family member you just put up with because you had to.

"Well, I'm going to stay here and watch the end of the sunset and finish my beer." Cindy was feeling... *what was she feeling?* Angry? Annoyed? Left out?

"That's silly. Come back with us." Vanessa rose in a graceful swoop.

"No, I'm going to stay awhile." Cindy held her ground. "I'll just walk back to the inn in a bit."

"Cynthia, I don't know why you have to be so

difficult." Her mother stood up, shook her head, and walked away.

"We'll meet you back at the inn, then." George turned and walked away after her family, dashing all hopes that maybe he'd stay with her and the two of them could have some couple time together.

Miss Tally came and sat down beside her. "Everything all right?"

Cindy looked out at the ocean for a moment, the sea awash with colors dancing across the surface. "I think so. I mean… I don't know what I mean." Everything was so confusing all of a sudden. She knew her family was—particular—but now she could see it was more bordering on snobbish and rude. And she didn't like that. And, even worse, George fit in with them beautifully.

"Miss Tally, I'm so sorry about my family and George. They were rude. I apologize."

"No use you apologizing. You didn't do anything wrong." Miss Tally reached over and took her hand. "You've always been the kindest, gentlest soul. I want you to be happy, Cindy. Does this fiancé of yours make you happy?"

Cindy looked into the woman's eyes. Eyes filled with warmth and wisdom.

"I think he does. I mean, he's perfect for me."

"Is he now?" Miss Tally stood up. "You make

sure before you commit to a marriage of just… convenience. A person should marry for real, can't-live-without-it love… and if you find that, you should never, ever let it go."

Cindy looked out at the brilliant sunset. George did love her.

He did, didn't he?

In George's own way.

Tally watched as Cindy stood and headed for the beach. A chill washed over her. The woman was heading into a heap of heartache, she could just feel it. She'd watched Cindy while the family was eating dinner. At best they ignored her, at worst her mother had nagged her to sit up straight and was appalled her daughter had ordered a beer. As if that was the worst thing a child could ever do to a mother…

Tally shook her head, chasing away the thoughts that always hovered at the corner of her mind. The doubts, the unanswered questions, the regrets. If she only had it to do all over again.

But, she was a practical woman. A person didn't get do-overs in life. You lived with the consequences of your actions, like she did every day of her life.

She wished she could do something for Cindy, though. Make her take a good long look at the biggest decision she'd ever made in her life so far. Marrying that fella. The one that Tally just knew in her heart was the wrong man for Cindy.

And the thing was, Tally knew who *was* exactly right for Cindy.

Cindy crossed the beach to walk along the shoreline. The sand had cooled with the sunset and a handful of couples walked along the beach in the fading light. She turned and headed back towards the inn.

The breeze had died down a bit and the gentle waves lapped at her bare feet as she trudged along the shore, thinking about what Miss Tally had asked. Of course George was the right man for her. He was perfect for her. Her family loved him and he wanted to spend his life with her.

She stopped her walk and sank down onto the sand, staring out into the ocean, mesmerized by the rolling of the waves and the sweeping arcs of the gulls, swooping by in the last light of the sunset. All this thinking was just bride-to-be nerves. It must be, because George was just... perfect. They were going to have a fabulous wedding. It was just like her wish she'd made all those years ago. It was all coming true. Just like she knew it would, because she'd never once doubted the power of making a wish at Lighthouse Point.

But she felt… off-kilter, somehow. She sat alone with her musings.

"Dream Girl." Jamie's low voice broke through her thoughts.

She looked up to see Jamie standing beside her.

"Mind if I join you?"

Cindy tossed a smile his direction. "Pull up some beach."

Jamie dropped to the sand beside her. "You looked lost in thought. I wasn't sure I should bother you."

"You're not disturbing me. I was just… thinking."

"You do that a lot. The thinking thing." He grinned at her. "You've got a couple of big days coming up, don't you?"

"I do."

"Are you just taking some quiet time alone? Or are you worried about the wedding? I'm sure Bella has it all under control."

"I'm sure she does. She's wonderful. Organized. And seems to be able to soothe my mother's ruffled feathers." Cindy sucked in a deep breath. "And her feathers are ruffled quite often."

Jamie laughed, his deep tones of mirth rolling over her, soothing her. His life was going well now. He wasn't making any big changes like she was. She was marrying George and going to spend the rest of her life with him.

So why did she feel the edge of panic taking over?

Jamie could see the hint of panic in Cindy's eyes. He'd never been great about talking about feelings, or hearing about someone's feelings, but darn it all if he didn't want to know what Cindy was feeling right this very minute.

"Dream Girl, what's up? Want to talk about it?"

Cindy stared out at the ocean, and he wasn't sure she heard him. She finally spoke. "I just feel… off. I'm not sure what's wrong. It's probably just wedding jitters."

"You sure?" Maybe Cindy was finally picking up on what a jerk her fiancé was. How he didn't treat her like she deserved to be treated. How this George fella was a pompous clown. But, of course he couldn't say any of that to Cindy.

"I don't know. I've never been married before, so I don't know for sure what wedding jitters are, but I do know I'm just jumpy or something. Miss Tally was asking some tough questions."

"She does that."

"She does. But... I mean... George is an excellent match for me. My family loves him. We know a lot of the same people. He seems to enjoy getting to know the people from our club in Lexington."

Jamie screwed up his courage and clutched a handful of sand. "But do you love him?"

"Well, of course I do. I'm marrying him, right?"

"Does he love you? Really love you?"

"Jamie, what has come over you? Of course he loves me. He asked me to marry him, didn't he?"

"I just want you to be sure, Dream Girl. I want you to be happy."

"Of course I'm happy. I'm getting ready to get married. I've dreamed about this day for years. It's just jitters, Jamie. Just jitters."

"Whatever you say." Jamie wasn't sure his voice sounded convinced. He *wasn't* convinced.

Cindy pushed off the sand and stood up. "Jamie, you need to back off. I'm fine. *Everything* is fine." She picked up her sandals. "I'm headed back.

I'll see you tomorrow." The curt tone of her voice was not lost on him.

Jamie let her walk away down the beach, knowing he'd pushed as far as he dared. But, he had an awful feeling that George was never going to give Cindy the life she'd dreamed of. He wasn't sure George was capable of thinking of anyone but himself.

Jamie sighed. He didn't know the man well. Maybe he was just making snap decisions about him. Cindy had to see something in him to want to marry him. Maybe he was just jealous of the man.

Wait. What?

Jealous?

No, he just wanted the best for his friend. That was all it was.

He was sure.

Fairly sure.

Well, pretty sure.

Jealous?

Jamie jumped up, brushed off the sand, and started trotting back to the inn. Too much thinking didn't ever do anyone any good. When he got back to the inn he noticed George and Henry were no longer at the fire pit with their cigars. Good. He'd rather not make friendly small talk with them.

He stood on the beach for a moment,

watching the waves in the moonlight. He loved this place. Loved the town, the island, the inn. He wanted nothing more than to make the inn a success and more profitable, supporting his mother by more than just scraping by each year like they had the last few years, watching every dime they spent. But, to be honest, even with worrying about the bottom line all the time, he and his mother had enjoyed the life they'd made here on Belle Island.

He turned to stare up at the inn. Light shone through many of the windows. A few people sat on the deck, illuminated by the torches that were lit each night. Yes, he loved their inn.

His gaze was drawn up to a room on the third floor. A man stood in the window looking out. A quick calculation told him that was the room George was staying in. A moment later, a woman came up beside him. Jamie's heart lurched. He did not want to watch George and Cindy.

He started to turn away, then realized the woman in the light had long blonde hair.

Not Cindy.

Alexis.

Maybe she had just brought up drinks to his room? Room service?

George leaned down close to the girl, his hand

rested on her shoulder, then reached up to close the blinds over the window and close out Jamie's view.

Jamie's pulse pounded in his veins. He clenched his fists. That rotten scoundrel. He was cheating on Cindy. *Probably*. The blinds had closed, but still.

Maybe Alexis was just bringing something up there. Maybe.

In cold, stony silence Jamie crossed the spread of sand and climbed the stairs to the deck. He grabbed some paperwork from his office and went to sit in the back stairwell on the third floor, because he was pretty darn sure Alexis wasn't going to trot down the main stairway when she left George's room. Unless she had innocently, well her version of innocent anyway, brought up an order to his room.

A few hours later Jamie's patience was rewarded. He heard the door to the stairwell open slowly. Quietly, Alexis slipped through the doorway.

"Alexis."

"Jamie. You startled me. What are you doing?"

"Waiting for you."

Alexis had the decency to look embarrassed. "How did you know… I mean, what for?"

"To fire you."

"Fire me? Why?"

"Why do you think? I can't have you causing

trouble with our guests. Come by in the morning and I'll have your last check ready for you."

"I wasn't causing… We were just… talking. You can't fire me."

"I just did."

Alexis brushed past him and hurried down the stairs. Jamie followed her out and pulled the outside stairway door closed firmly behind her. He'd rather be short staffed than have Alexis anywhere near George.

The solid click of the door echoed in the stairwell, mocking him and forcing him to make decisions he didn't want to make. Should he tell Cindy? Of course he should. She had a right to know. But she'd told him to basically back off. He should respect her wishes.

Shouldn't he?

CHAPTER 10

Tally readied the table in the far corner by the beach. It was Friday morning and Josephine and Paul would be by for coffee and a cinnamon roll at nine. The restaurant wasn't open then, but they had fallen into the habit years ago. Paul would drop by and they'd have their Friday morning coffee together. Now Josephine joined them.

Tally looked forward to their visit. She and Paul had been friends for many years. He'd been there for her when no one else was. He'd helped her make hard decisions. She knew she was one lucky woman to have a friend like that. They'd never been romantically inclined over the years, neither one of them would chance messing up the friendship, she guessed. Now Paul was married to his childhood sweetheart, and Tally couldn't imagine a more perfect match for him. The two of them were ridiculously in love and it made her smile just to see them together.

She looked up and waved as she saw Josephine and Paul weave their way through the aisle to their table. Tally poured them each a cup of coffee, grabbed some cinnamon rolls, and set the food on the table. She knew that Josephine would pour a bit of cream in her coffee and Paul would drink his black. They'd both have a cinnamon roll, and Josephine would only eat half of hers, giving Paul the remainder. Each week was the same. Tally liked that. The predictability. The routine.

"Has anyone heard from Susan?" Paul set down his cup.

"Jamie has. He said she was having a fabulous visit with her sister, but was starting to get anxious to head back home. I think she feels guilty being gone for the big wedding weekend."

"You knew the bride from when she was a child, didn't you?" Josephine asked.

"I did. She used to run around with Jamie. They were great friends. Always up to something." Tally sighed. "I'm not sure she's making a good decision with this George guy though."

"Bella thinks the same thing." Josephine nodded. "She thinks he's all wrong for Cindy."

"I tried talking to her when she was here last night. Not sure I got through to her, but at least I hope I got her thinking carefully." Tally shook her head. "Her family is something else. They weren't very happy about much here at Magic Cafe and made sure everyone around them knew it."

"Oh, dear." Josephine's eyes clouded with concern.

Paul laughed. "As if anyone who comes here cares about what some out-of-towners think about Magic Cafe. You know we all love it, Tally. And you." He winked at her.

Tally smiled. "Always my biggest supporter, aren't you Paul? You know I'd never had been able to make a go with Magic Cafe without all your help at the beginning."

"We had some tough times didn't we? Me, trying to start the gallery, and you the cafe."

"And between us having about a thimbleful of business knowledge."

"But look at you both now." Josephine swept her arm wide. "You both have successful businesses here in town, and you've both helped Julie open The Sweet Shoppe and helped Susan with her decisions about the inn."

KAY CORRELL

"Julie is still struggling a bit with her shop, but at least her life is looking all rosy with her engagement to Reed. I sure like that young man." Tally took a sip of her coffee.

"He does seem like a fine fellow. Any news of a wedding date? I want to make sure Josephine and I are in town for it." Paul looked at Tally.

"Nothing yet. I think Julie is still a bit shocked with everything and not trusting her own happiness. She just needs time." Tally glanced around the cafe, noticing the early workers arriving and setting up the tables. "Now if Susan and Jamie can get the inn so it runs more profitably. They both work so hard. Her brother kind of let things slide for a while, but it seems like they are slowly climbing back up."

Tally reached for the tray of cinnamon rolls and took one herself. "I'm not sure that this wedding party appreciates the atmosphere of the inn, though. I think they are more of the fancy-shmancy, club-type people. Well, not Cindy. She's a good, down-to-earth girl."

"Well, while you ladies solve all the problems in town, I'm going to dig in and enjoy my breakfast. Julie makes the best cinnamon rolls. I'm glad you decided to get them delivered each day once Julie stopped baking for you and opened The Sweet

Shoppe." Paul took a large bite. "Still the best roll in town."

"Hi, y'all."

Tally looked up and saw Susan making her way over to them.

"Susan! You're back." Tally jumped up and gave the woman a hug.

"Just got in town. I got up early this morning and drove in from my sister's. I called Mandy yesterday and heard she has the chicken pox. She said that your great-niece was helping with the wedding, Josephine."

"Bella. She is. She's really enjoying it. She's a planner, that one."

"Well, I figured Jamie could use a hand with everything. To be honest, I hated missing the wedding weekend. It's the first big one we've had since Jamie and I took over the inn."

Paul stood up and held out a chair for Susan. Tally went and grabbed another coffee cup.

"I'm sure Jamie will be glad to see you." Tally handed the cup to Susan. "Did you have a nice visit with your sister?"

"I did. But, to be honest, a little goes a long way. She chatters all the time. Wants to go, go, go… and I just wanted a little break from how hectic our life is now."

"You need to find a better person to vacation with. Someone who likes to take it easy. Sit and read. Relax." Tally laughed. "So it would never be with me. I'm fairly certain I don't know how to relax."

"As if you ever take a vacation." Paul grinned. "Though, I think one of these days we're going to talk you into one."

"Maybe." Tally could hear the doubt in her voice.

"So, tell me everything you know about the wedding, the bride, the family." Susan took a sip of her coffee and looked expectantly at Tally and Josephine.

The women obliged her with all the details they knew, while Paul sat patiently enjoying his cinnamon roll.—and then the second half of Josephine's roll as usual.

"Mom, what are you doing back so soon?" Jamie came from behind the counter, gave his mother a hug, and reached to take her bag out of her hand. He'd hoped she'd come back looking all rested, but no such luck. Though, she did look happy to be home.

"I couldn't stand missing the wedding. I know it was a good time to visit my sister for her schedule, but not so much for ours. I talked to Mandy—"

"Mom, you did not have to come back. I have it all under control."

"I know you do. Mandy said as much. Said you have Josephine's niece helping you."

"Bella. She's great. I don't know what I would have done without her."

"Well, I'm here now to help in any way I can. I'll help Dorothy at the desk today. I know we have a full inn of people checking in. That will free you up for whatever else you need to do."

Jamie had to admit he was relieved. He could use the help. So many loose ends. So many things to check on for the wedding. The wedding where Cindy was marrying the cheating jerk.

Cindy had made it clear that he was to stay out of her relationship with George. But did she know that George was a cheater? Was she knowingly entering into a marriage of convenience? No, that couldn't possibly be what Cindy would want.

"You okay, son? You look lost in your own little world."

"What?" Jamie looked at his mother. "No, I'm okay. Just puzzling out a few things. I'll put your bag in my office. I'll bring it over to our cottage in a bit."

"Thanks, sweetie." His mother headed behind the reception desk right as Dorothy entered the lobby.

"Susan, you're a sight for sore eyes. We can use another set of hands around here this weekend."

"Glad to be here."

"So, had enough of your sister, did you?" Dorothy winked.

His mother laughed out loud. "You know me too well. Yes, I love her, but really I need to remember a couple of days is way long enough for a visit. She's a constant whirlwind of activity."

With that, the door swung open and a large group of people crowded into the lobby.

"I'll leave you two with this. Call out if you need me, I'll be in the office. Oh, and I hired the Hawkins brothers to help with luggage and anything else you need them for this weekend. They should be here any minute."

Jamie walked into his office, feeling guilty he was so glad he wouldn't have to work the front desk today. He wasn't feeling up to plastering on a fake smile and putting up with people who he was afraid were going to act as entitled as Cindy's family did. His mother was much better at handling people. He much preferred the behind the scenes running of the inn.

The stagnant air of the office stifled him, and he crossed over to throw open the window. The air-conditioner had been blasting out air for days. He was much more a fresh air type person. There was a nice breeze this morning, so he'd just let the office air out a bit before the expected heat of the day descended upon them.

He sat at his desk, doing some bookwork he'd been avoiding with the busyness of the wedding snaring all of his time. Voices drifted up from below.

One voice caught his immediate attention.

George.

What the heck was he doing out on the patio under the window? Jamie couldn't help himself. He walked over to the window to peek down. He gritted his teeth as he saw George downstairs talking to Alexis.

"I'm sorry you got sacked. I am. Last night was fun, but it was just that. Fun."

Jamie clenched his jaw, then spun back toward the doorway when he heard someone enter.

Cindy.

Not good. Not good at all.

"Have you seen Bella?" Cindy asked, totally

oblivious that her world was being torpedoed right below the window.

"Jamie?" Cindy cocked her head, looking at him curiously. "What are you looking at?"

"I. Uh…no. I think she said eleven, right?" He glanced at his watch.

"Calm down." George's voice drifted through the open window.

"Is that George?" Cindy crossed the room.

"I can't have you messing things up. Don't go getting all hysterical." Every single word of George's was crystal clear.

Cindy stood frozen by the window, her face a mask of disbelief.

"I'm sorry Jamie fired you. But it's probably for the best you aren't around this weekend. I don't need the distraction. I have a good thing going here. Marrying into a prominent Kentucky family. Good connections. It's time for me to settle down. It's good for my career. My firm isn't big on promoting bachelors, they think we're not steady enough." George's laugh drifted through the window.

Jamie watched as Cindy reached out and clung to the window sill. He took a step closer, but she shook her head. His heart pounded in his chest, feeling every bit of the pain Cindy was feeling.

Wanting to fix it. Wanting to hold her and take her pain away.

"Don't you love her?" Alexis's young voice drifted upwards.

"Love? What does love have to do with it? That's some kind of schoolgirl fantasy. I'm fond of Cynthia. Marriage is like a business deal. You marry the person who will bring the most to the table." George laughed again.

Cindy spun on her heels and walked towards the door.

"Cindy, wait."

"No, leave me alone, Jamie. Stay out of it. Please. Just leave me alone."

At that moment, Jamie knew his heart was breaking for Cindy. And the reason it was able to break? Because he was afraid he was falling in love with her.

Cindy sat on the edge of a chair in her room staring at... nothing. Nothing at all. She rolled around George's words and didn't know any way to make them be anything else than what they were. She was a business deal for him. A merger.

He'd said he was fond of her. *Fond*. What a silly word.

But fond meant he *cared* about her, right?

But he didn't love her. Though, maybe George didn't really know what love was. Surely he loved her. He did. Sometimes men just had a tough time saying the words out loud. He'd asked her to marry him so he *had* to be in love with her.

He'd showered her with gifts and spent every weekend with her. Granted it had mostly been at parties and business events and rarely just the two of them.

When was the last time the two of them had done something alone? She couldn't remember.

A heaviness settled over her, squeezing her heart and constricting her breath.

She jumped up from the chair and paced the room. She knew that pretty young blonde had been flirting with George and that George had enjoyed it.

She was certain that was all it was. A harmless flirtation.

But the sting of his words burned through her as she paced back and forth.

Bella grabbed a cup of coffee in the cheery breakfast nook of Aunt Jo and Paul's kitchen. "Um. I love that first sip of coffee in the morning."

"Do you want something to eat, dear?" Aunt Jo sat at the table, back from her weekly breakfast at Magic Cafe. Her aunt got up way too early, as far as Bella was concerned. Though, to be honest, Bella's two boys got her up way too early, too. But she'd been enjoying sleeping in a bit on her vacation this week.

"No, just coffee. Thanks. I need to hurry up and get over to the inn. Check on a few things before I meet with Cindy."

"Rumor around town is her young fella seems a bit… stuffy, doesn't he?" Aunt Jo raised an eyebrow.

"Well, he's certainly not the kind of guy I'd pick, but to each his own, I guess. I just wish he acted like he was, well, in love with her. Maybe it's just the stress of the wedding though."

"Maybe." Aunt Jo's voice didn't sound convincing. "Have you thought of talking to her about it?"

"Oh, I couldn't do that. I'm just the coordinator, not her friend."

"Well, I don't see anyone else here in town that is her friend."

"Her sister is here."

"The one I heard told her that her dress made her look frumpy? That sister?" Aunt Jo shook her head. "You know, you might be doing her a favor if you just were a sounding board for her. Let her sort out her feelings a bit. Make sure she's making the right decision."

Bella sighed. "I don't make any promises, but I'll try. I've grown fond of her and I do want her to be happy. You know me, I'm a sucker for a happily-ever-after ending." She took one last sip of coffee and set the cup in the sink. She reached down and kissed her aunt. "I'm probably going to be gone all day. I'll see you later, sometime after the rehearsal."

Bella hurried out of the cottage and drove to the inn. The parking lot was busy with people arriving for the weekend. Wedding guests, she presumed. She crossed the lobby, deftly avoiding luggage and people chatting in groups.

She spotted Cindy talking to two young women. Cindy waved her over, but seemed quite distracted.

"Bella, these are my bridesmaids... my cousins."

Bella smiled at the meticulously dressed pair of identical twins. "Nice to meet you."

Twin one smiled briefly, but twin two didn't bother to answer. "We're going to go find Vanessa. She said we could go shopping this morning."

Bella thought that maybe the maid of honor and bridesmaids would be all about helping the bride today, but she guessed not.

"Okay, have fun." Cindy nodded at the twins and turned to Bella. "Want to come up to my room? I'm afraid if we stay down here we'll have constant interruptions as people arrive for the wedding."

"That's a good idea."

They headed up to Cindy's room and sat at a small bistro table by the balcony. Bella opened her notebook and Cindy opened her planner. They both went through their lists, checking things off as they made sure everything was ready. Cindy seemed to just mechanically go through the motions though, and it worried Bella.

Bella closed her notebook with a flourish. "I think we're ready."

Cindy turned and looked out at the ocean. "Yes, we're ready."

"Are you okay?" Bella reached across the table and touched Cindy's hand.

Cindy turned and looked directly at her. "Do you think people get married for all sorts of reasons?"

"Probably. But I'm a firm believer in marrying for love. Marrying your best friend, someone who acts like they are so lucky they married you. Someone you can talk to, share your deepest secrets." Bella looked across at Cindy. "Why do you ask?"

"Well… I'm not sure that George and I have the same views on marriage. I guess this is kind of late in the game to be thinking about that, isn't it?" Cindy's voice was low.

"It's never too late. You can change your mind right this minute if you're not sure about things."

"I'm… Oh, I guess I'm just having jitters. George isn't the romantic type. I'm sure he cares about me."

Bella sat silently, letting the woman talk.

"He's the ultimate person for me, though. He is. He and my father are great friends already. That's good, right? Mother adores him and brags to all her friends about what a catch he is." Cindy smiled sheepishly. "I'm pretty sure she never thought I'd settle down and get married. She'd given up on me. Then along came George."

"How do you feel about George?"

"Oh, I'm in love with him, of course. I'm marrying him, right? He's good to me. I do wish he were more romantic, but what man is, really?"

"My Owen is romantic. Very."

"Then you are a lucky woman. Anyway, enough

of this. I've known what he's like from the very beginning. We're very compatible. He accepts my faults. I accept his."

"Just make very sure that you're making the right decision, for the right reasons." Bella sat quietly and watched Cindy stare out at the ocean, lost in thought. She only hoped the woman took time to really think about the decision she was making. Bella was fairly certain this was more than just wedding jitters.

CHAPTER 11

Julie drove her van over to the inn. She ran inside to the lobby, looking around for Reed. No sign of him. She turned to the reception desk.

"Susan. You're back." Julie smiled as she hurried over to the desk.

Susan came out from behind it and gave her a big hug. "Just got back. Heard about Mandy having chicken pox, and figured Jamie needed me."

"So, you had enough of your sister, huh?" Julie grinned.

"You and Tally. You know me so well." Susan shrugged. "My sister means well, she just thinks there always has to be some event each day. I just wanted a do-nothing vacation."

"Well, glad you're home. We'll have to catch up after this weekend."

"I hear Reed found a place to rent."

"Yes, you should see it. It's gorgeous, huge, right on the beach… and the kitchen. Man. I could live in that kitchen."

Susan laughed. "A gorgeous kitchen is the way to your heart, huh?"

"The direct route." Julie laughed.

Susan moved behind the reception desk again. "Reed said he'd be down in a minute. That pile is his." She pointed to a stack of suitcases and bags.

"We're going to get groceries, and I'll haul him over with his things."

"There he is." Susan nodded towards the stairway.

Reed came up, pulled Julie into his arms, and planted a kiss on her lips. "Missed you."

"You just saw me this morning when you came by for coffee." Julie smiled.

"That was hours and hours ago, trust me." Reed kissed her again.

"Okay, you two. Go get Reed all settled into his new place, though we'll miss having him here."

"I can't thank you and Jamie enough for everything you did for me these last few months. I loved staying here."

"We loved having you."

With obvious reluctance, Reed let Julie go and crossed over to scoop up his things. Julie grabbed a few of the bags and they headed out to the van.

After picking up staple items, fresh fruit, makings for lunch, and other assorted groceries, they headed for the beach house.

Julie was still a bit shocked with the size of the house and the knowledge of how much the rental was each month. Reed insisted it was the house he wanted though, so who was she to second guess him… and there was the fabulous kitchen.

Reed led the way to the front door, unlocked it, and threw open the door with a flourish. Julie slipped inside and went straight to the kitchen. Reed carted everything into the house, while Julie began unpacking things and putting them away in the pantry and the fridge, marveling at the space with what she knew was a silly grin on her face.

Reed smiled as he watched Julie. She stopped once and touched the red knobs on the stove. It was almost a caress. He figured she'd enjoy cooking in this state-of-the-art kitchen. At least he hoped she would. Julie turned toward him and smiled.

"I love this kitchen."

"More than you love me?"

"No, but close." She grinned.

"Harry lined me up with weekly cleaning service, too. I'll need that. I'm not the world's best housekeeper."

"You better keep this wonderful kitchen clean."

"I'll try my best, ma'am."

"Why don't you go unpack your clothes, and I'll make lunch. We can eat out on the deck."

"That sounds great." He wandered through the house and into the massive master suite. A four-poster bed was positioned against one wall, with French doors on another wall leading out to the deck. He dumped his clothes out of the suitcase and made quick work of putting everything away. He stored the suitcases in the back of the walk-in closet and moved into the bathroom to put away his toiletries. The master bathroom had a huge walk-in shower and a whirlpool tub, as well as a double vanity. Nice. He put his things away and wandered off to decide where he'd set up his office.

A smaller bedroom with a trundle bed, on the road side of the house, had large windows and a small screened porch off of it. That would work perfectly. He'd just need to find a table and he'd set up here.

Maybe after he bought a car, he'd go to one of the many flea markets around here and pick up an old desk.

If he got a car.

He still wasn't ready to take that step yet. He'd been taking driving lessons for a while now. Trying to get more confident with driving again since the accident he'd been in that had killed his wife. He was determined to overcome his fears and get back behind the wheel. He wasn't going to be a burden on Julie, with her hauling him around all the time, and somehow he didn't see her as the type of person to be comfortable with him hiring a full-time driver for them to use.

He had a perfectly good car sitting in his three-car garage back in Seattle, but there was no way he was going to drive it across the country. He could hire someone to drive it here, but he'd been researching car safety and planned on getting the safest one he could find.

He wandered back into the kitchen and walked up behind Julie, standing at the stove. He wrapped his arms around her and nuzzled her neck. She smelled of fresh lavender. She leaned back against him as she stirred the pot on the stove.

He kissed her neck and she laughed. "I need to finish up. Go and set the table outside."

"I'd rather stay her and kiss your neck."

She shooed him away with a dish towel and he obligingly went about the table setting chore he'd been assigned. He glanced back inside to see Julie efficiently dishing up their meal, a smile on her face. He could just stand here and watch her for hours.

He didn't know what he had done to deserve this woman, but he knew he was one lucky man.

CHAPTER 12

J amie looked out on the beach, checking to make sure the beach workers had set up enough chairs and umbrellas for the arriving guests. They'd given all the wedding guests early check-in times today, so they had quite a gathering on the beach. Far down the beach he saw her. Cindy. He knew just where she was headed. Lighthouse Point. Her thinking spot. Her refuge spot. The place she used to go when her sister had teased her one time too many, or her mother had corrected her posture-hair-dress-whatever criticism of the moment.

He waffled briefly. Let her go alone, or catch up with her and try to talk to her. With a shrug, he leapt off the side of the deck and trotted down the beach after her. He really should leave her alone. That's what she'd asked. He argued with himself the whole time he trailed down the beach after her, keeping his distance.

Leave her alone.

Go talk to her.

He rounded the bend on the long, sweeping point. The lighthouse stood looking grandly out to sea. There she was on a small outcropping of rocks, sitting and watching the ocean, her knees tucked up under her chin, her arms wrapped firmly around her legs.

The thinking pose.

With a burst of nerve, telling himself he was doing the right thing, he swung up on the rocks beside her and sat down.

"Dream Girl." He reached out a hand and touched her face. A lone tear tracked down her sun-kissed cheek.

"Jamie." She leaned her shoulder against him, ever so slightly.

"What can I do?" Helplessness washed over him. Wanting to help her, but knowing she had to sort things out for herself. Jamie wanted to tell Cindy about seeing George with Alexis in his room and wanted to say George was just marrying her for her money. But he knew, deep in his heart, he couldn't be the one to crush her dreams. He just couldn't.

"I'm so confused." She still didn't look at him, her gaze was lifted up to a gull swooping through the sky.

"Talk to me."

"I know George doesn't feel the way about me that I always thought a groom would feel. He's not romantic. I've known that from the start. But he is fun. He gives me little gifts for no reason, or big things like that car of mine." She paused and played with a small shell she held in her hand. "He does care about me. He does in his own way, I've known that from the beginning. I've just always filled my head with these romantic notions of what marriage and weddings were like. He'll be a good husband for me."

Jamie sucked in a breath of the humid sea breeze. "Do you love him?"

"I'm in love with him."

"Not quite the same thing, is it? Are you in love with him, or are you in love with your idea of the perfect wedding? Or is it the fact your family likes him and he fits in so well with them? You need more than that for a happy marriage."

"But I am happy when I'm with George."

"Are you?"

"Of course. I wouldn't marry him if he didn't make me happy."

"But you should have so much more than that in a marriage. So much more. You deserve more. You should have someone who thinks the sun rises and sets with you. Someone who wants to spend all his time with you. Talks to you. Shares things with you. You should be able to talk about anything with him." He paused for a moment. "He should be your best friend."

"I think not all marriages are like that, Jamie."

"They can be." He emphasized each word. "They *should* be."

"I sometimes think you're about as hopelessly romantic as I am, Jamie. But I've grown up. Everything is not always hearts and roses." She looked out at the waves once again. "Besides, the time for doubts is long past. I'm marrying George tomorrow."

"He's not good enough for you, Dream Girl."

"Oh, Jamie, I'm surprised he even wanted to marry me. Look at me. I'm creeping up on forty years old, a klutz, my hair is always impossible, and I carry extra pounds around so I can never pull off that smartly-dressed style. I'm pretty sure Mother and Father had given up on me ever marrying."

It tore at his heart Cindy had such low self-esteem. But who could blame her with the constant criticism from her parents and sister? "Cindy, you are smart and funny and beautiful. You just don't see those things. Any man would be lucky to have you."

"Ah, Jamie, you've always been my biggest supporter. I've missed that. You're good for my ego, you know."

"I say the truth." He touched her face again where the tear had long since dried in the salty sea air. "You are a wonderful woman, kind-hearted. It isn't too late to change your mind about George."

But with that sentence he was nailed with a pang of guilt. Did he really think George was wrong, or did he want Cindy for himself?

Of course George was wrong.

He was a cheater. He practically ignored Cindy at every turn.

But he couldn't deny it was killing him now that Cindy was back in his life, to think of her spending her life with George.

Spending her life with any other man…

Cindy didn't know why everything had to be so confusing. She liked things all sorted out and well planned. She organized her whole life in her planner. So, why was everyone telling her to think twice about marrying George? The rehearsal for the wedding was tonight, for Pete's sake. George was a catch. He was. And she cared about him. Sometimes she even thought she loved him. She was sure the feeling would grow after they were married. They were very compatible. They were.

Yet, why was it so easy to sit with Jamie, talk to him, and tell him how she felt? He was just so easy to be with. She'd missed that. The effortless friendship. He never judged her, never teased her about her weight, her hair, or her lack of style. He didn't give her the eye when she ordered a beer.

She looked over at Jamie and he met her gaze. "If you think George is so wrong, how come you've been working so hard to make this wedding perfect for me?"

He didn't flinch, but took her hand in his. "To be honest, I need this wedding to go off without a hitch. I need to build up the wedding business at the inn to help make the inn more profitable. We're always a bill away from losing the place."

"I had no idea things were so shaky for you and your mom."

"We have a reporter from Florida Destination Weddings magazine coming. If we get a good write-up, it will help a lot. I need to pull this off. I need to give Mom some more security after Russell left her... well, without anything. She worries about the finances all the time. I keep thinking we're so close to turning the corner, then something else hits and clears out any savings I've managed to scrape together. A busted air-condition system, damage from a hurricane, a new roof. It's always something."

"Jamie, I'm sorry. I never thought that the inn might be in trouble. It's such a figure here on Belle Island."

"Well, if I can't make a go of it, I'm sure some developer will swallow it up and put up a condo complex. An inn like ours is a dying breed here."

"But it shouldn't be! It's so charming and relaxing and the perfect place to come and stay."

"Don't suppose you'd like a PR job here, huh?" Jamie smiled wryly.

"Well, we'll just have to give that reporter a wedding like she's never seen, won't we?"

"No, we don't. Not if you want to cancel it all."

Cindy stood up. "I don't want to cancel. I've just been having foolish, schoolgirl thoughts. Jitters. That's all." She reached down a hand to Jamie. "Come on, we should head back. I'm sure you have better things to do than sit here and listen to me ramble."

"I always have time for you, Dream Girl."

"You're a good friend, Jamie McFarlane. A really good friend. I've missed you. You've always been the only one I could talk to like this. Thanks for listening to me. I feel better. I do."

She was determined to put all this foolishness out of her mind. She had a mission. To pull off the most perfect wedding this reporter had ever seen. Concentrating on that would push all this silliness from her mind. She'd do that for Jamie.

George looked down the beach and saw Cindy walking towards the inn with that blasted Jamie fellow. Annoyed, he glanced down at his watch. Shouldn't she be up getting ready for the rehearsal? It took a woman some time to get ready for big events like that, didn't it? He hoped she did something with her hair and really, *really* hoped her mother had talked her into an appropriate dress. He couldn't wait to show her off to his groomsmen and for them to meet her father. They'd see how well he was marrying.

To be honest, if he'd known her sister was

WEDDING ON THE BEACH

available when he'd started dating Cindy, he might
have made a move for Vanessa instead. But, by the
time Vanessa was disentangled from her husband,
George had already been dating Cindy for a few
months. He was quite sure her father wouldn't have
approved of a quick sister swap. Vanessa was more
his style in a woman, if a bit critical and hard. And
she did love to spend money, a lot of money. But,
she carried herself well and always looked
impeccable.

Ah, water under the bridge. He'd chosen the
other sister. When she put the effort into it, she was
able to make quite a presentable showing. He'd
bought her an expensive necklace he planned to
give to her. That would impress the heck out of his
friends.

Cindy and Jamie walked up the steps to the
deck and he stood watching them carefully. Jamie
had a hand on her elbow as they climbed the
stairs. Probably to keep the woman from tripping.
She did have a tendency to stumble with
regularity. He only hoped she didn't fall at their
wedding.

When the couple got to the top of the stairs,
Cindy stopped and gave Jamie a quick hug.

George didn't like that. Not one bit. What was
she doing hugging another man? That Jamie was

just entirely too familiar with her. Or she was too familiar with him. Or something.

The irony of being jealous wasn't lost on him.

George crossed the deck in time to see Cindy look up guiltily.

"Ah, there you are darlin'. Been looking for you. Isn't it time for you to go up and get ready for the rehearsal?" He leaned over and kissed her.

Slowly.

On the lips.

Right in front of that Jamie fellow.

"I. Ah. Yes, I was just coming back from my walk. It *is* time to go up and get ready."

"You'll excuse us?" George used his best dismissal tone with a nod toward Jamie.

"I have work to do, yes." Jamie gave Cindy a long look, then crossed the deck and slipped inside.

"I hope you didn't get your face all burned in this sun. Don't know how you'd cover that up. You look a bit red." He peered at her closely.

"No, I put on lotion. I'm fine. It's probably just a bit flushed from the walk and the sea breeze."

"What was he doing with you?" George nodded towards the door Jamie had gone through.

"He was out walking on the beach, too. We walked back from Lighthouse Point together."

"I see."

She looked at him curiously. "You aren't jealous, are you? Jamie is just a friend."

"Jealous? Of course not. Don't be silly."

She placed her hand on his arm. "George, you do love me, don't you?"

"Where is all this foolishness coming from? Of course I do. I asked you to marry me, didn't I?"

"You're right. I'm just being silly." She reached up and placed a quick kiss on his cheek. "I'm going to head upstairs now. I'll see you at the rehearsal."

George watched as she crossed the deck. Women were funny things. You always had to keep reassuring them. Well, the necklace he was giving her would show her, for sure.

He turned on his heels, put Cindy and her silly questions out of his mind, and headed to the bar to have a drink with his friends.

CHAPTER 13

Cindy crossed the lobby to where Jamie stood talking to a woman with a camera bag slung over her shoulder. Jamie waved her over.

"Cindy, this is Jackie from Florida Destination Weddings magazine."

"Nice to meet you, Jackie."

"Nice to meet you, Cindy. I'm going to be taking some photos of the set up for the rehearsal, along with some photos of the wedding set up and reception. Would love to have a few of the bride and groom. If that's okay, I have a release form for you to sign."

"Is that all fine with you?" Jamie looked worried.

"Yes, that's fine." Cindy signed the paper and handed it back.

"I have your room all ready for you too, Jackie, if you want photos of our accommodations"

"Sounds great. I want some photos of the inn, to give our readers a feel for what the venue is like."

"I'll show you up to your room, then."

Cindy watched as Jamie led the reporter away from the lobby.

"Cindy?"

She turned at the sound of her name. A woman came out from behind the desk and walked up to her. "I'm Susan, Jamie's mom. You probably don't remember me. I only visited a few times in the summers even though Jamie was here each summer helping my brother."

"I was sorry to hear about your brother passing away."

"Thank you." Susan nodded. "He was my only sibling, and it was a hard loss."

"I do remember meeting you, though. You came for a long weekend with Russell, but he left early."

Susan smiled softly. "Russell wasn't one to really want to vacation. At least not down here. He likes fancy resorts with a hubbub of activities. He's not really a beach person either."

"I don't know how anyone could keep from falling in love with this place. The inn. The town. The beaches here."

"You're sweet to say that." Susan looked around the lobby and back to Cindy. "It's nice to see the inn full of people coming for your special day. I hope you have a beautiful wedding here."

"I'm sure I will. And I just met the reporter. I hope she does a great article for the magazine and it brings you more wedding business."

"I do, too. Jamie is very hopeful. He's done so much with the inn. I'm afraid my brother had kind of let things slide. Jamie is bringing things around."

"Well, I love this place. I can't think of a more perfect place for a wedding."

"Thank you for saying that. If there is anything I can do for you, just let me know." Susan turned and headed back to the reception desk.

Cindy stood in the middle of the lobby, knowing she should go upstairs and get ready, and fighting off the urge to race out the door and back down the beach.

Silly girl, with a silly case of nerves. She squared her shoulders and headed upstairs. She was going to put aside this nonsense and pull off the perfect wedding. For herself, for Jamie and his mother—

and for George—she guiltily added him as an
afterthought.

~

Jamie led Jackie up to her corner room on the second
floor. He'd saved one of their nicer rooms for her. He
hoped to impress her, he'd admit that. He opened
the door to the room and Jackie stepped inside.

"Just set my suitcase by the door. I want to get
some photos of the room and the view before I
unpack and mess things up. The room is lovely."

Jamie had made sure to fill the room with
flowers and a basket of chocolates, cheese and fancy
crackers, along with a nice bottle of wine. He wasn't
above bribery for a good write-up.

"Can I get you anything else?"

"No, I'm fine for now. Thank you. Your inn
really is lovely."

"Thank you. We think so."

Jamie pulled the door closed behind him and
walked down the hallway. He fervently hoped he
could pull this off. He took the stairs to the lobby
and crossed over to where his mother was working
behind the counter.

"I just met Cindy again."

"I was going to introduce you."

"Well, I re-introduced myself. She seems like such a lovely girl."

"She is."

"Well, I hope her wedding brings you the publicity you're wanting."

"Me, too, Mom. Me, too."

But as much as he wanted the good publicity, he didn't know that he wanted the wedding to actually take place. Because that would mean that Cindy really was marrying George.

And he was all wrong for her.

Cindy heard a knock at her door and crossed the room to answer it. Vanessa stood in the hallway. Her sister brushed past her and entered the room.

"Are you about ready?" Vanessa eyed her critically. "Do you want me to do your hair for you?"

"I thought I'd just wear it down tonight." Cindy had clipped one side of her curls back with a fancy comb with lavender stones on it that matched the trim on her dress.

"Are you sure? It's going to be a fly-away mess

before long." Vanessa scrunched up her face in obvious displeasure.

"I'm sure."

"Why not just pull it back with an elastic rubber band, then?" Vanessa rolled her eyes. "Really. It's the rehearsal for your wedding. You'd think you'd want to look… put together at least."

Cindy ignored her sister for once. She thought her hair looked nice pulled slightly back like this. She wasn't going to let Vanessa's steady stream of negativity dampen her spirits.

Cindy took one last look in the mirror and turned to her sister, wanting to ask the question, but not sure her sister was the right person to ask. She screwed up her courage and blurted out her fear. "Vanessa…do you think George loves me?"

Cindy could tell that she'd asked the wrong question to the wrong person, before her sister even answered.

Vanessa shrugged her shoulder and flicked her hand with a you're-so-ridiculous flip of the wrist. "Don't be silly. Maybe he does, maybe not. I'm not sure it matters. He cares about you and wants to marry you. Marriage is give and take. The whole marry for love, one true soul mate is just a fantasy. This is the real world. This is how it works."

Cindy wasn't reassured a bit from that taste of sisterly wisdom.

"Anyway, you're lucky he asked you to marry him. It's not like you had a lot of other prospects. You don't want to just grow old alone do you?" Vanessa checked her reflection carefully in the mirror. "I sure don't. I plan on getting serious about dating again after we finally make it back to Lexington."

Cindy didn't want to grow old alone, she didn't. She wanted to share her life with someone. But it wasn't like she'd even been out looking for a husband. George had found her. George had asked *her* out. He'd asked *her* to marry *him*.

"You're not getting cold feet are you?" Vanessa eyed her suspiciously. "Getting wrapped up in one of your fantasies again?"

"No. Just a bit of wedding jitters, I think."

"Well, pull yourself together. We have lots of important people here. We don't want to keep them waiting."

Cindy almost laughed. The last thing Vanessa ever worried about was keeping people waiting.

CHAPTER 14

Bella looked around the outside eating area on the deck. Cindy had chosen to have the rehearsal dinner outside, but the wedding reception tomorrow in the inside dining room. Tonight, the dining room was for wedding guests who were not part of the actual wedding party and rehearsal. Tomorrow the dining area, inside and out, was reserved for the wedding.

Bella walked over and straightened up a place setting at one of the tables. A long buffet was set up along one end of the deck. The Tiki bar area would have the drinks, along with servers walking around with Champagne. She checked with the staff to go over the schedule for the wedding. So far things were going as planned.

Jamie walked out onto the deck and waved. He stopped by the bar, then came over to stand beside Bella. "Everything going okay?"

"All in order." Bella nodded towards the Tiki torches lining the deck. "You have those set to be lit at dusk?"

"I'll be lighting them myself."

"Looks like things are getting busy at the inn this evening."

"I think most of the wedding guests who are staying here are checking in today. We've had a constant stream of people coming in all day. The dining room is filled with reservations for the night, for guests who aren't part of the wedding party. Might be able to squeeze in a few without reservations, but not many." Jamie furrowed his brow. "I just hope everything goes off without a hitch."

"It will be fine. I'm sure," Bella reassured him.

Just then one of the boys Jamie had hired to help with the luggage came running up. "Jamie, your mother told me to come get you. The hot water is out in the inn."

Jamie's eyes clouded with exasperation. "That's not good. I better go see what I can do." He turned to Bella. "You've got this out here?"

"I do. Good luck with the water thing."

Jamie nodded and hurried into the inn.

"Harry, I can't thank you enough for coming over on short notice. Couldn't get ahold of our regular repair guy, and this is just out of my league." Jamie grabbed a toolbox from his best friend's truck. "I'm more of a paint, patch, and fix than anything mechanical."

"Glad to help if I can."

Jamie and Harry had been friends since Jamie's first summer on Belle Island. Harry lived in town year-round. Once Jamie had moved back to take over the inn, the two of them had resumed their friendship. Harry knew more about fixing anything and everything than anyone Jamie had ever met.

"Come on, let's go check it out." Harry grabbed another toolbox and followed Jamie to the maintenance room.

Harry poked around and checked things and finally came up with the verdict. "Looks like you just ran out of hot water. Too many guests getting ready at the same time, I guess."

Jamie raked his hand through his hair. "That's not good. There'll be even more people getting ready at the same time tomorrow. I'm going to have to get another water heater system put in here, aren't I?"

"If you want to keep having the inn full for big events where everyone hits the showers at the same time."

"Well, I can't have that finished by tomorrow." Jamie sighed in frustration. "And I sure don't have that in the budget for this year, either."

"Well, you can ask the guests to spread out their showers, or realize you're going to have angry guests that are going to have to take cold showers." Harry slapped Jamie on the back. "Cheer up, old man. It could have been that the whole water heater system had gone out. I've turned the temperature up to the max allowed, that might help some."

"I guess there is that one bright thought, it wasn't replacing this one and adding a new one."

"You've done a lot with the inn so far since you took it over. These things take time."

"I'm worried that we're running out of time." Jamie tried to push back the wave of discouragement. No time for a pity party now. There was a wedding to pull off. Even if it involved cold showers for everyone.

"Wish I could help you with that." Harry picked up the toolbox.

"Wish you could, too. But thanks for the help

on the water heater. Sorry to pull you away from your Friday plans."

Harry laughed. "My hot Friday plans involve a cold beer and doing some more work on that cottage I'm rehabbing."

"Right now, that sounds like a perfect way to spend the evening." Jamie picked up the other toolbox, followed his friend out to the parking lot, and helped him load up his truck.

"Thanks again." Jamie shook his friend's hand. "I owe you."

"And I'm keeping score." Harry winked and climbed in his truck. "Call me when you get a night off. We'll go grab a drink."

"Sounds good. Thanks." Jamie waved to his friend as he pulled away.

He walked back inside and overheard a couple at the front desk. "There is no hot water. How are we supposed to get ready for tonight?"

"We're working on it right now. I'm sure it will be fixed soon." His mother was patiently soothing the guests. "Here, have a complimentary glass of Champagne."

His mother looked up as he came up to the desk. "And?"

"Harry said it looks like we just ran out of hot water. We're going to need to put in a second system if we're going to have events with this many people getting ready at the same time."

"That's not good." His mother's forehead wrinkled with concern. "We don't have that budgeted at all."

"That's just what I said to Harry. We'll have to look over the budget and see what we can put off, so we can add the new water system." Jamie looked over at the dining room where it was beginning to fill with early diners. "I better go in there and help with things. There should be more hot water soon. I'm not sure what we'll do tomorrow when even more people are getting ready at once for the wedding."

"Well, it is what it is, son. We'll make do."

Jamie didn't like the feeling of defeat that was washing over him. This whole perfect wedding was turning into one disaster after the next.

Bella led the rehearsal for the wedding. The wedding party gathered around and she passed out glasses of Champagne for everyone to sip while she read through the timeline for the ceremony.

They did a quick run-through of which

bridesmaid walked with which groomsman, and where the parents would sit.

"Okay, this is where you and your father walk down the aisle." Bella nodded at Cindy.

Cindy didn't know why she was so nervous. It was the rehearsal, not the real thing. Her father looked at her questioningly. "You okay?"

"I'm fine." Cindy settled her hand on her father's arm. They walked out the door and down the steps to the aisle between where the chairs would be set up tomorrow. Towards the arbor where George stood joking with his friends. He turned to see her right as she managed to catch her heel on something in the walkway and tumbled down to the sand.

She took a hard fall and the breath whooshed right out of her. Bella came rushing forward, and her father bent down over her. "Are you all right?" Her father's voice broke through her concentration of trying to get a gasp of air.

She pushed up off the sand to her knees. Such a graceful entrance...

George strode down the aisle towards her, she could see his Italian leather shoes get buried in the sand as he walked.

She bet that annoyed him.

Then his leather-clad feet were right in front of

her face. He reached a hand down for her, and she took it. He tugged her to her feet, and turned to his groomsmen. "I told you she fell hard for me."

The men laughed and George leaned down close to her ear and whispered, "I hope you can manage to walk all the way down the aisle tomorrow without falling. Seriously, Cynthia, your constant clumsiness is embarrassing."

The flush of heat flooded over her face. She could see her sister and mother standing by the arbor, Vanessa shaking her head in exasperation. She fought to get air back into her lungs.

"Are you okay?" Bella leaned close with an anxious look in her eyes.

"I'm... fine." Cindy steadied herself, then withdrew her arm from George's clasp. She dusted the sand from her dress and turned to her father. "Okay. Let's go on."

"It is hard walking on this sand, isn't it?" Her father smiled at her. "I'll make sure I keep better hold on you now. You just lean on me."

"Thanks, Dad."

She managed to walk the rest of the way to the arbor and stood by George while the minister ran through what he would be saying, in what order.

"You want to practice kissing the bride?" The minister winked at George.

George laughed, grinned at the groomsmen, and planted a long kiss on her lips. The longest kiss he'd given her since he showed up, she realized with a start, and it seemed to be all in show for his buddies.

George grasped her elbow and turned. "Let's go all the way back inside without falling, shall we?"

She could hear the groomsmen laugh behind her back as she and George headed back inside. Her face flushed with embarrassment again.

As they walked inside the inn, Cindy turned to George. "I'm going to run and freshen up. I'll be back in a minute." She turned and hurried—carefully—down the hallway and pushed into the quiet sanctuary of the small library. She sank onto a settee and tried to catch her composure and recover from her total humiliation.

CHAPTER 15

Jamie watched Cindy slip away and followed her to the library. He'd seen her take the tumble down the aisle and had wanted to rush to her side. His mother had been standing next to him and had placed her hand on his arm and shook her head. He'd watched helplessly as that jerk fiancé of hers had made jokes at her expense.

He opened the door to the library and slipped inside. He knelt down before her and took her hand. "I saw what happened. Are you hurt?"

"Just my pride."

"Ah, Cinderella Dream Girl. It was just a little tumble."

"In front of everyone. I'm such a klutz. George is furious with me. I'm pretty sure he's embarrassed to be marrying a woman who falls at every opportunity."

"Don't be so hard on yourself."

"Oh, Jamie. You know how I am. I'm constantly tripping. I'm not sophisticated and fashionable like most of the people who will be here at the wedding. George is probably regretting his decision to ask me to marry him."

If only that were true and the jerk would back out of the wedding.

Wait, what?

He didn't want Cindy to get hurt. But he didn't want her to marry the man either. He wasn't good enough for her. She deserved so much more.

"I think you are one of the most fascinating people I have ever met. You look beautiful in that dress you're wearing tonight, by the way. I like your hair down like that, too."

Cindy gave him a weak smile. "You're just saying that to cheer me up."

"Nope. Saying it because it's the honest truth."

"I know I said it before, but you're a good friend, Jamie."

"So are you, Dream Girl. So are you." He stood up and reached a hand down for her. "You ready to face the crowd again?"

"I think I am. Yes, I am." Cindy smiled a

genuine smile then, just for him, and it made his heart soar before he could even stop himself.

He purposely ignored his heart and walked her to the door of the library. "You have a good night. This should be a special time for you. Enjoy yourself."

She nodded, slipped out the door, and headed down the hall. It didn't escape his notice that her steps were hesitant.

He realized, even if he didn't like to admit it, that he did want her to enjoy herself. He wanted her to have this special time, enjoy her wedding and the festivities around it.

If only it wasn't with George.

Cindy crossed through the dining room and looked around at all the guests enjoying their meals. She realized she only knew a handful of the people there. Most were business associates of her father or George, even the people outside at the rehearsal dinner. How had it come to this? A handful of family members. Her cousins as bridesmaids. Where were her friends? Where were the people she knew?

She had a lot of acquaintances and people she

crossed paths with over and over, but where were her true girlfriends? She'd lost contact with most of the women she'd hung out with in college. She'd never been that popular in high school, though she'd tried so hard to fit in. She'd thrown parties at the club, swim days at her parent's pool, and had girls over to go riding. She was always invited to parties in high school, too. But she often thought it was more because of who her parents were, than that the girls really wanted her there.

A sadness seeped through her, which was silly considering she was getting ready to marry tomorrow. Perhaps all women reexamine their lives before taking such a big step.

She looked over at George, laughing with his friends from college and the friends he'd made in Lexington. She envied that, the easy way he made friends wherever he went. She'd just never been like that. She was always afraid that she didn't quite fit in with any crowd.

George looked up right then and saw her staring at him. He gave her a little smile and raised his glass in a silent acknowledgement and turned back to his friends. Her cousins came bustling up to her.

"Did you just about die when you tripped?"

"Aren't you afraid you'll fall tomorrow, too?"

"Wonder what George thought? It was so embarrassing."

"I would have wanted the earth to open and swallow me up if that happened to me."

Cindy didn't even bother to answer the questions. Her cousins had a way of yammering without really expecting an answer. Thankfully, they turned their conversation to talking about eligible bachelors attending the wedding.

She silently watched her cousins as they chattered away, and she realized she had only asked them to be in her wedding because they were the cousins closest to her in age. *She didn't even like them much.* How was that for an ungenerous thought? They were self-absorbed and... well... shallow.

She'd thought that marrying George was going to be the magic key to acceptance from people in their world. But, she was beginning to realize, it wasn't really going to make much difference. She was going to go from being invited to things because of her parents, to being invited to events because of George. She had to admit to herself, she did like going places with George. It was easy to go to things with George, the simple act of being on his arm had made her feel accepted and part of the crowd.

But look at her, at her very own rehearsal dinner. Reduced to standing alone and listening to her cousins go on and on and never including her in the conversation after their first recriminations about her fall.

Bella came outside and walked over to her. "You look so pretty tonight, Cindy. I like your hair like that."

"Thank you." Cindy reached up and touched the fancy comb in her hair.

"Things seem to be going well. Jamie just told me they'll start serving the buffet in about five minutes. If you want to go get George, I thought it would be nice for the bride and groom to go first."

"I'll go get him." Cindy crossed the distance, realizing the rehearsal dinner party had been going on for over an hour, and she and George hadn't spoken a word. She touched his arm as she came up to stand beside him. He acknowledged her with a brief smile, but continued on with his story he was telling his buddies. When he came to a stopping point, after the requisite laughs from the groomsmen, Cindy interrupted, "The buffet is ready. We're supposed to start the line."

"Let's get your parents to go with us, then we'll start."

That was nice of George to think to include her

parents. He did think of little nice things like that quite often. She should appreciate the little things more, instead of focusing on imaginary problems and feeling sorry for herself.

They filled their plates with all kinds of tantalizing dishes. Local fish, fresh salad, hush puppies—she had insisted though her mother didn't think they were fancy enough to serve—and tiny fruit tarts and chocolate bonbons for desert.

Cindy, George, and her parents crossed over to the table reserved for them. George pulled out her chair for her—see he did do the nice little gestures —and she moved to sit on the offered chair. Her heel caught on a board on the deck and she started to fall.

It all happened in slow motion, she swore it did.

She reached out a hand to steady herself and grasped at George's arm… the one where he'd balanced his plate of food. Cindy went tumbling to the ground, along with her plate of food and George's… which managed to spill all down his pants leg.

"Cynthia. Honestly." Her mother's voice drifted over, etched with embarrassment and recrimination.

The tears sprung up in Cindy's eyes. *Not again. Not like this.*

Bella came rushing over. "Are you okay?"

Cindy nodded, unable to speak.

George stood in judgmental silence, glaring at the food dripping down his leg. "I'll go change." He walked away without so much as offering Cindy a hand.

Bella wrapped her arm around Cindy and helped her up. "Come with me." Bella whispered in her ear. Cindy clung to the woman's arm and followed her away from the table and the staring eyes. Bella paused for a moment and turned to her father. "Go ahead and get the guests started eating. We'll be back soon."

"She's okay?" Her father's voice held concern.

"I think so. We'll just take a few minutes to pull ourselves together."

Bella kept her arm around Cindy as she led her into the inn. "Let's run up to your room and get you cleaned up."

In the room, Cindy let the tears continue to fall, not even trying to stop them.

"It's okay, you know. It was just a fall."

"The *second* fall of the evening," Cindy said between gulps of air.

"I wish I could make you feel better. Tell you it was okay. I know you're embarrassed." Bella went to the bathroom and came out with a wet towel. "I actually think George got the worst of it.

Let me see if I can get that spot out of your dress."

"George is furious with me."

"Well, it's kind of silly to be mad at someone because they tripped, isn't it?"

"He says I'm always a klutz and doing things that embarrass him. I can't believe I fell again." Cindy's heart pounded in her chest, her face burned in embarrassment, and she didn't think she could go down there and face everyone again. Ever again.

Later that evening, Cindy sat on the cool sand and gazed out at the ocean. She picked up handfuls of sand and let the grains sift between her fingers. Moonlight spilled across the ocean, dancing across the waves. She was almost certain most people didn't spend the night before their wedding sitting all alone on the beach.

The ocean breeze cooled the streaks of tears trailing down her cheeks. She couldn't believe how the rehearsal dinner had turned out. It was nothing like she'd planned. Nothing like she'd dreamed.

She'd tripped down the aisle. She'd dumped a plate of food all down George's pants. He was mad at her and didn't even try to disguise it. Her mother's eyes had shone with barely disguised disgust. She was positive everyone at the rehearsal was laughing at her or pitying her. It was not exactly what she expected from her perfect wedding.

She wondered if she would even be able to walk down the aisle tomorrow without tripping. She knew all eyes would be on her. They were probably even taking bets on whether she could make it down to the arbor without tripping. She dashed away the tears on her face, not liking the pity party she was having but unable to pull herself out of it.

She had to admit that it hurt the way George had treated her. Instead of being supportive, he'd made fun of her. Instead of helping, he'd stepped away to change clothes.

She dug her heels into the sand and repeatedly pushed them away, digging troughs in the sand. She plucked up a lone shell and turned it over and over in her palm, admiring the perfect edges, and wondering how long it had been in the sea. If she hadn't picked it up, how long would it be until it was ground into grains of sand? With one last look at the tiny shell, she tossed it into the sea.

She heard the scrunch of sand as someone approached. She hoped whoever it was walked right past without saying a word. She didn't feel like being friendly. But the footsteps stopped right beside her and Jamie dropped down on the beach.

"Hey, Dream Girl. Here we meet again." Jamie covered her hand with his own.

Her hand lingered in a sandwich between the cool sand beneath it, and the warmth of Jamie's hand above it. "Hi" She didn't really feel like talking yet, but it was nice to have Jamie by her side.

"I hear you had kind of a rough evening."

"You could say that." Cindy laughed bitterly "I managed to fall twice. George is furious with me. My mother thinks I made a fool of myself and she's probably right. Vanessa keeps saying I'm lucky George doesn't walk away."

"I don't think you should listen to them. It's not the end of the world, even though I'm sure it feels like it. Nobody likes to be made fun of." Jamie reached over and tucked one of her flyaway curls behind her ear "I'm not sure why they were picking on you. That's pretty mean-spirited."

"After my second tumble, I would've liked the ground to just swallow me whole like my cousin suggested."

"I sure would miss you if the ground swallowed you up." Jamie smiled at her and squeezed her hand.

"And it's not only that I've made a supreme fool of myself." Cindy sniffled back more tears. "I'm ruining everything for you. I know you need the recommendations. A good write-up in the magazine. I'm just... ruining it."

"You haven't ruined anything."

But Cindy knew she had dashed any hopes of people from George's crowd recommending the inn as a wedding venue. Between George down-talking the place, and her tripping, falling, and spilling... things hadn't been very impressive so far. She knew that wasn't fair to Jamie and his mother, because none of this was their fault.

She squared her shoulders and dashed away the last of the tears.

The last of them, silly woman.

She was going to find a way to turn things around for Jamie. Point out all the lovely things about the inn. She was going to be a one woman PR person for him tomorrow and also after she got back to Kentucky.

You know, along with getting married tomorrow.

"I probably should go upstairs and try and get some sleep." Cindy brushed the sand off her dress.

Jamie jumped up and reached a hand down for her. She took it and let him slowly pull her to her feet.

"Thanks." She swished her hands together, knocking off some more sand. She turned to look at the inn. Lights shone from a handful of the windows. Laughter drifted down from the large deck, lit only by Tiki torches. She hoped Jamie and his mother could find a way to save the inn. It was such a grand old place to stay, a charming surprise among the polished and generic hotels and condos along the beach.

She loved this inn with her whole heart.

She turned to Jamie. "I need to get something from my car, before I go up to my room."

"Here, we'll go around the side. It will be quicker than up and through the inn."

Jamie took her elbow and led the way through a break in the dunes, along a narrow pathway towards the side of the inn's property. They came up to the corner of the inn and Cindy saw a couple lounging on a small patio near the kitchen entrance.

She felt Jamie stiffen by her side and glanced up at him. She followed his gaze over to the couple on the dimly lit patio. She heard George's low voice and a young woman's laugh. That waitress. *What was her name?* Alexis.

Cindy stood, trapped, unable to move. She watched the scene, like a bystander would watch a train wreck she couldn't stop. The woman stretched up and placed a quick kiss on George's lips.

He didn't pull way, he just laughed his ever-so-charming laugh.

"Hey now, I'm going to be married tomorrow." George's voice drifted back to where Cindy stood frozen in place.

Cindy heard, rather than felt, the quick gasp of breath she took.

Jamie reached out for her elbow and steadied her.

"Well, you could have one last night of fun." The woman sashayed in front of George.

"That's mighty tempting, young lady. Mighty tempting." George stood in the low lamplight.

Surely he'd say no and go inside. It was just the girl flirting with him. Right?

The girl brushed up closer to George, wrapped her arm around his neck, and planted a good long kiss right on his lips.

George wrapped his arm around the girl and pulled her tight.

Jamie pulled away from Cindy's side and strode along the side of the inn and up to the patio. Alexis pulled back in surprise while George let out a low laugh.

"You're just everywhere, aren't you Jamie boy?"

"Alexis. Why are you here? I fired you."

"I was just stopping by." The young woman stood her ground.

"You were just leaving." Jamie stood between George and Alexis. "Oh, and as a rule, I don't encourage my *fired* employees to kiss the groom-to-be the night before his wedding." Jamie voice held more than a tinge of anger.

"It was just some harmless flirting." George's voice spilled over with the tone of superiority that annoyed Cindy.

"Alexis, you should leave." Jamie stood there until the young woman walked away.

"Cindy is too good for you." Jamie turned toward George and shook his head.

"It was just a kiss. Anyway Cindy's chosen me and you can quit being her protector. She's mine. She's marrying me tomorrow."

"Not if I can talk her out of it." Jamie walked back towards where she was hiding in the shadows.

"You can't talk her out of it. She loves me." George tossed the words after Jamie's retreating back.

Jamie returned to where Cindy stood in the shadows and took her hand. "I—"

"No. Don't say a word. Not a word." Cindy pulled away from Jamie and ran back across the sand to the deck. She brushed past the partiers and fled into the inn and up to her room.

Only when she reached the safety of her room did she take in a deep breath of air. She flipped on the lights and looked around the room, not seeing anything. She sank to the floor, her back to the door, and hugged her knees close to her chest.

Jamie stood at the corner of the inn, watching Cindy rush away from him. He froze in place, staring out into the night. Cindy's pain had been palatable. It had spread over him, squeezing his heart, like the betrayal had happened to him, not to Cindy.

He'd half expected her to go marching up to George and tell him it was over.

She was going to tell George it was over, wasn't she?

She couldn't possibly marry the man. He was a cheater, that was obvious. And a pompous jerk. She deserved so much better than that.

He couldn't stand by and let her throw her life away. Even if it's what her mother and family wanted for her.

He stood for a moment and wrestled with the

hard truth, not quite willing to let the thoughts fully develop.

He sighed then and gave up.

He couldn't let her marry George, because—

Time to admit the truth, old boy.

Jamie scrubbed a hand across his face. The truth was—and he could just now admit it—*he* was in love with Cindy. He couldn't bear for her to marry another man... much less that blockhead of a man, George.

CHAPTER 16

The next morning, his wedding day, George stood in his room, still annoyed at that Jamie guy for catching him with Alexis. He'd hoped to have a bit of fun last night, but Jamie had squashed his plans. Who could deny a man his last bachelor night fling?

Jamie had probably gone straight to Cynthia with his tattle telling. George needed to do something to smooth things over.

Now would probably be the perfect time to give Cynthia her wedding present, the way-too-expensive necklace. But he'd had to spend that much, both to impress her father and make his friends think he was doing better than he really was. He considered it an investment. Besides, soon he'd be married into the Pearson family. The sky was the limit then.

He crossed over to the desk in the room and pulled out a sheet of stationery from the drawer. He sat down and glanced at the page for a moment, then started to write in his precise, strong handwriting.

Dear Cynthia,

Just a small token of my affection for you. I look forward to becoming your husband this evening. I know I have my shortcomings, but I appreciate how you understand me and take me as I am. You know you are the only one for me. I'm so glad you said yes and I can't wait to be married.

Love,

George

There, did that sound like something a woman would want to hear? The take me as I am line should work on her guilt and sense of obligation if Jamie did talk to her last night. The whole *only one for me* line was pretty good too, if he did say so himself.

He sealed the letter and went to find his best man to deliver it, and the necklace, to his bride-to-be. For some reason, the woman believed in that crazy tradition of not seeing the groom on the day of the wedding before the ceremony. Well, he'd humor her today.

He opened the door to his room and ran into Vanessa. Oh, even better than giving it to his best man. Vanessa would be sure to tell her parents about the necklace.

"Vanessa, could you do me a little favor? Won't take you long."

"What is it?" Vanessa looked a little unsure. He couldn't blame her, she probably had a million little details to wrap up as the maid of honor. He paused for a moment and looked critically at Vanessa. A fine looking woman. Always so well put together. She seemed to truly enjoy all the social obligations and functions her family went to. It's too bad Cynthia wasn't a bit more like her sister, but surely he could get her to change over time. One thing he wanted to do was to buy her a whole new wardrobe. After the marriage, they'd be invited to all the big events in Lexington and around on the big horse racing events. They needed to make a good impression, a super-couple if he had anything to say about it. He'd waited a long time to find the perfect match, he just hoped Cynthia didn't mess that up for him.

He was fond of the woman. She was intelligent

and had some charming friends he'd gotten to know. Well, not quite friends, but acquaintances.

"The favor?" Vanessa's voice broke through his thoughts.

"Yes, I have this present for Cynthia. I wonder if you could bring it to her room for me. She doesn't want me to see her before the wedding."

"Ah, that's our Cynthia. Always lost in one of her fantasy versions of life." Vanessa shook her head. "Yes, I'll drop it off now."

"Thanks, Vanessa. I appreciate it."

He watched as Vanessa headed down the hall to Cynthia's room and smiled to himself. Hopefully the necklace would get him firmly back in Cynthia's good graces if that Jamie character had tried to interfere.

Cindy woke up to a stream of sunshine flooding in through the window. She glanced at the clock and saw it was already after eight in the morning. How could she have slept in so late? She had so much to do.

Her wedding day!

She rolled over, pushed up, and sat on the side of the bed, excitement rushing through her.

Then she remembered.

She remembered *everything*.

All the events from yesterday came flooding back. Tripping at the rehearsal and again at the dinner. George kissing the waitress.

She flopped back down on the mattress and threw an arm across her eyes, blocking the sunshine, blocking the memories that taunted her.

She lay motionless on the bed until a knock at the door broke through her thoughts. With a sigh, she pushed up off the bed and went to answer the door.

Cindy opened the door and Vanessa pushed into the room. "The humidity here is going to ruin my hairdo today. Can it get any muggier?"

"The breeze is supposed to pick up this afternoon. That will help blow some of the humidity away." She'd been obsessively checking the weather all week. It looked like it would be ideal weather this evening.

"I heard they are low on hot water. I took a shower early this morning so I wouldn't be caught taking a cold one later." Vanessa walked over to the mirror and looked at herself. "Unless, of course, I die of heat stroke before the ceremony even begins."

Cindy went back and sat on the bed, waiting for her sister to end her litany of complaints.

"Oh, before I forget. George gave me this to give to you." Vanessa reached into the large leather handbag she was carrying and handed Cindy a small wrapped package and an envelope.

Cindy stared at the obviously store-wrapped gift.

"Aren't you going to open it? Go ahead. See what it is." Vanessa stood expectantly beside the bed.

Cindy pried open the envelope and pulled out the letter. She read it quickly. George was always a good one with his words.

"Open it." Vanessa nodded towards the present.

Cindy slowly untied the ribbon on the box and unwrapped the present. A pretty emerald-green jewelry box was emblazoned with the name of the most renowned jeweler in Lexington. She pried the box open and gaped at the diamond necklace. It was exquisite. She'd give him that.

Vanessa squealed. "Oh, look at that. It's gorgeous. It must have cost a fortune." She reached out for the box. "All those diamonds! Here, try it on."

Vanessa pulled the necklace from the box and Cindy obediently pulled her hair up so her sister could fasten the necklace. She got up and crossed to the mirror and locked eyes with the stranger looking back at her. The diamonds encircled her throat and glistened in the light.

"You are one lucky woman." Vanessa's voice held a tinge of awe. "That is gorgeous." Vanessa stood beside her.

Cindy looked at her sister's reflection in the mirror. "It is pretty. He does have good taste in jewelry."

"That's all you're going to say about it? He has good taste in jewelry? You are wearing a fortune around your neck. Wake up. You've caught the most eligible bachelor of the century."

Cindy reached up to touch the stones. "I've been thinking about that."

"About how lucky you are?"

"Thinking about George." Cindy bit her lower lip.

"Don't bite your lip like that. So unattractive." Vanessa shook her head. "Wait a minute. Someone is at the door."

Her sister crossed the room and swung the door open. "Mother, come in and see what George just gave Cynthia."

Cindy watched her mother cross the room, impeccably dressed in a light blue linen suit with shoes that cost over a month's salary for most of the real world. Here she was, slipping into her mother's world, where zeroes didn't seem to matter on the price of things… or maybe the zeroes were all that *did* matter.

"Cynthia, that necklace is just perfect. Look at it. You must be thrilled. That George is a keeper. You're so lucky."

"I was just telling her that." Vanessa sank onto the bed. "But she was just about to tell me what she's been *thinking* about."

Her sister said the word "thinking" like it was a sure sign of crazy.

"I said I'd been thinking about George." Cindy started the subject tentatively.

"Well, that's good. You're marrying him today." Her mother picked at a mythical piece of lint on her skirt.

"That's the thing." Cindy summoned up her courage.

Vanessa eyed her suspiciously. "What's the thing?"

"Last night I caught him kissing that young waitress. Or she was kissing him, but it's not like he stopped her."

"Don't be a goose. It was probably just one of those last-night-of-being-a-bachelor things."

"He flirts with a lot of women."

"But, for some unknown reason he chose you,

didn't he? So, what's your problem? Men are like that anyway. Anything flashy catches their eye. Marriage is more like a... business arrangement. You need to marry someone compatible. Someone who runs in your same circles." Vanessa jumped up and went over to stand beside Cindy. "You need to realize, he might flirt a bit. That's okay, but with any luck, he'll still come home to you."

"What if that's not enough?" Cindy's heart pounded in her chest. "I'm just not sure."

"Of course you're sure. You can't embarrass your father and me like that, by changing your mind *now*. We have business associates here, our friends. It's time to stop living in your fantasy world. George is a good catch." Her mother crossed the floor with precise steps on her very high heels. "You need to quit this ridiculous talk."

"Mother, I'm confused. Worried. Sometimes I'm not even sure he's in love with me."

"Of course he is. Look at that diamond necklace he just gave you. That says he loves you."

"Does it?"

"You are the most frustrating sister of all time." Vanessa flounced back across the room and sat on the bed. "I will never understand you. Look at that necklace. Of course he loves you."

"I don't know how I feel about him anymore.

He was so... non supportive when I fell yesterday. Like I did it on purpose to embarrass him."

"Well, you did embarrass him in front of all his friends and our friends." Her mother arched an eyebrow.

"I didn't mean to. I just... tripped."

"Yes, well, let's try not to do that today, okay?" Vanessa rolled her eyes.

"Cynthia, you need to stop this nonsense now. You're just having normal bride nervousness. Put it out of your mind. Promise me." Her mother turned away before Cindy even had a chance to answer. "Come on Vanessa. We should give Cindy time to shower and get ready. The hairdresser will be here soon."

"We talked you out of all this craziness, didn't we?" Vanessa paused with her hand on the doorknob. "You'll quit the over-thinking thing?"

Cindy nodded, because she'd learned long ago that it was easier to agree with Vanessa and her mother than not.

"Good. We'll see you soon." Vanessa swept out of the room with her mother right behind her.

Cindy sat on the bed and stared at her recently manicured nails and the glittering diamond ring George had given her for their engagement. She reached up and touched the diamond necklace.

Now this. His way of asking for her forgiveness? By way of an apology?

True, he hadn't even said he was sorry or asked for forgiveness. He probably didn't even know she knew he'd kissed someone else last night. Kissed Alexis for longer than he'd kissed her any time since he'd gotten to Belle Island. Maybe longer than he'd ever, ever kissed her.

CHAPTER 17

Susan gathered her courage and knocked on the doorframe of her son's office. "You got a minute?"

"Pretty jammed up right now, can it wait?" Jamie glanced up from his desk. "I'm running down the checklist for the wedding."

"No, it can't wait." She entered the office and closed the door behind her.

"Okay, what's so important?" Jamie's eyes shone with a bit of aggravation for the interruption. She knew him well. He was trying to keep himself busy today. More than busy. So he could ignore what was really going on.

"I think you should tell her."

"Tell who, what?"

"Tell Cindy." She pinned him with her best mother stare over the top of her glasses.

Oh, good. It still worked—her son squirmed a bit in his chair.

"Tell her what?" He kept pretending he had no idea what she was saying.

"Have you told her how you feel about her? I can see it. Anyone can see it. If you don't tell her now, it's going to be too late."

Jamie sat still as a statue then let out a long whoosh of air. "Mom, she's getting married today."

"You don't see George looking at her the way you look at her, do you?"

"I can't just go up to her and blurt out my feelings."

"Why not? What do you have to lose?"

"Some things are better kept to yourself." Jamie had his stubborn, I-won't-change-my-mind look plastered on his face.

"Some things aren't." Susan sat in the chair across from her son. "Sometimes you have to risk it, to take a leap of faith. It's worth it if you find real love."

"I assume you're not talking about Russell."

Susan flashed a wry smile at her son. "No, not Russell. But your father, he was my true love. I thought I could make myself care about Russell like

I did your father. You saw how well that worked. I did try with Russell, I did. I'm afraid that Cindy is making the same mistake as I did. Marrying for the wrong reasons."

"I never did know what you saw in Russell."

"Russell was safe. I had you to consider and support."

"You never should have married him for my sake."

"It wasn't only for you. It was… well, it seemed like the right decision at the time. I never could make Russell happy or live up to his expectations."

"Neither of us could. Nothing I did was good enough, I could never please him."

"I know, and I'm sorry for that. At least you know that I've always been proud of you."

Jamie gave her a small smile. "Thanks, Mom."

"And now you should listen to my advice. True love is the real reason to get married. The kind where you can hardly stand to be apart. Where your heart trips when you see them." Susan sighed. "I had that with your father."

Susan leaned forward. "I just want to point out that people marry for a lot of reasons… or just happen into a marriage because of timing or family pressure or wanting a child. But the really lucky people in this world find someone who can be their best friend, support them when times get rough, be there for them and with them. Love them unconditionally." Susan stood up and walked behind the desk and kissed her son on top of his head. "That kind of marriage, that kind of happiness, that's what I want for you."

She turned and headed for the door. "So I think you should take that risk and tell Cindy how you feel. Take a chance that you'll find that kind of happiness."

Jamie sat at his desk, staring off into space after his mother left. She was right. *Probably*. He should go talk to Cindy and tell her how he felt. George was never going to make her happy. He was going to cheat his way through their marriage. George was that guy, Jamie just knew it.

But it was Cindy's decision to marry him or not. Not his.

But if he didn't at least go tell her how he felt… took the risk… would he regret it his whole life?

He looked up to see Bella standing in the doorway.

"Things going okay? Anything I can help you with?" Bella smiled at him, then a frown creased her brow. "You okay? You look... like you've seen a ghost or gone through an earthquake... or something."

Jamie let out a bitter laugh. "My mother's been here with motherly advice. She wants me to take a risk. To tell someone the truth."

"She wants you to tell Cindy how you feel about her?"

Jamie looked up in surprise. "How did you know?"

Bella laughed. "I've known since the first time I saw you two together. The way you look at her. The comfortable way you two are with each other."

"But she's marrying George."

"That's the plan for today."

"But she saw him kissing someone else last night. And still... she didn't confront him. She just let it go."

Bella arched one eyebrow. "That's a bit of a shocker. Well, not so much about George. He's a ladies' man, through and through. He looks at them and undresses them with his eyes. He's that type. Knew it the first time I met him, too. I'm surprised Cindy didn't go deck him, though."

Jamie sighed in frustration. "I thought for sure she'd kick him to the curb. But as far as I know, everything is still on for her wedding."

"So, are you going to go talk to Cindy?"

Jamie pushed away from his desk and stood up. "I don't know. I don't think so. I mean, the one thing she wanted was a perfect wedding. Somehow, I don't think that includes another man professing his feelings for her."

"You might regret it if you don't at least try."

"I might… but I feel like Cindy needs to make the decision to marry George or not… decide if he's right or not… without me interfering. I want her to come to that decision on her own."

"You have a point there."

"I just don't think it's the right time for me to speak up."

"As long as you realize, it's now or forever hold your peace." Bella turned and walked out of his office.

He stared out his window, more confused than ever.

Forever hold his peace.

Bella knocked on the door to Cindy's room. She heard some noise inside, then the door opened. Cindy's eyes were swollen and it was obvious she'd been crying.

She also was wearing the most exquisite diamond necklace with her tank top and shorts.

"Oh, Cindy. Are you okay?"

"Just peachy." Cindy walked back and plopped on the bed. "I'm pretty sure George has cheated on me, more than once, actually, and I've just ignored it. I caught him kissing someone last night… which my mother and Vanessa insist was just a last night of bachelorhood thing. But… I'm just so confused."

"I'm sorry." Bella sat on the bed next to Cindy and let her talk.

"And George gave me this lovely note and this beautiful necklace today." Cindy touched the diamonds encircling her neck. "Yet… I just feel like… running away. Which is ridiculous because he's actually the perfect match for me."

"Is he? Well, I'll tell you something. I married the first time because it was expected of me. Married the guy I dated through high school and I'm glad I did, because I got two great boys out of that marriage. But we were so wrong for each other. He wanted me to be something and someone I just… wasn't. I couldn't ever quite measure up in his eyes." Bella reached out and touched Cindy's hand. "But I'll tell you something else. Then I found my Owen. He is my everything. My best friend. And one look from him makes me melt.

He's my biggest cheerleader and staunch supporter of anything I try. Even cooking—I'm terrible at it—and he just smiles and eats it and says it's great. I can't imagine going through life without him. My heart swells inside just thinking about him. That...*that* is what real love is like."

Cindy looked at Bella with troubled eyes. "That's what I always imagined marriage would be like. I imagined my wedding would be so perfect. And now..." Cindy looked away. "I don't know what to do."

"Only you can make that decision. You need to listen to what your heart tells you." Bella hugged Cindy. "I feel like we've become friends this week. I wished you lived in Comfort Crossing. You'd love my friends Jenny and Becky Lee."

"You know, I feel closer to you than anyone I've invited to this wedding. Thank you for everything you've done for me this week, and thank you for being my friend."

Bella stood up. "You let me know if I can do anything. Let me know what you decide. I support any decision you make."

CHAPTER 18

Vanessa and the bridesmaids left the dressing room and Cindy stood in front of the mirror, looking at her reflection. She circled slowly in the wedding dress her sister and mother had chosen for her, in the heels that were as uncomfortable as they were ridiculous for walking down a sandy aisle.

She looked at the dress with its sleek lines and tight fit. She hated everything about it. She hated the updo the hairdresser had starched into place. She hated the too dark eye shadow the makeup artist had applied and reached over for a tissue to wipe it from her eyelids.

Yet, she knew that she looked like just the bride that George wanted in this dress, with this fashionable hairdo, with the flashy makeup and designer shoes.

Only… it wasn't her. This woman in the mirror was some figment of everyone else's imagination.

A bride befitting a business merger, just like George had said.

But that wasn't what *she* wanted.

She didn't want a husband who cheated on her and ignored her, who made fun of her when she tripped. She didn't want to feel like she needed George so she could feel like she fit in.

With a growing realization, she acknowledged the fact she didn't *care* if she fit in anymore. She'd tried so hard to fit into a life that she really didn't even want to have. Tried to make herself into the person her mother wanted her to be… only Cindy didn't want to be that person.

She leaned down and slipped off the ridiculous shoes.

She heard a knock at the door and crossed the room to open it.

"Dad."

"Oh, Cynthia, you look so beautiful, so elegant…" Her father paused and crinkled his brow. "And so… uncomfortable."

"I…" Cindy couldn't even find the words. "Dad, I'm sorry. It's all wrong. So very, very wrong."

Her father stood silently for a moment then reached out for her hand. "You know, sweetheart, I've lived with this silly fear that you'd marry someone who wasn't worthy of you. When George came along, I was so pleased. I like the man. He fits in well. But you know, I don't think he is worthy of you. I can't abide a cheater and I'm pretty sure he is one. I admit to sometimes looking for worthiness in the wrong places. I want nothing more than your happiness. So you do what you have to do."

Her father gave her a hug. *A hug*. She couldn't remember the last time he'd hugged her. Or spoken that honestly with her.

"Dad, that means so much to me. Your support."

"Your mother and Vanessa can be an overwhelming force, I know that very well. I should have stood up to them more with their constant haranguing of you over the years." He let out a long sigh. "It's sometimes just easier not to cross your mother, though. I do love her. I think she means well in her own way. It just makes our marriage run smoother if I go along with her. But I should have put an end to this nonsense of picking on you all these years. I'm sorry. You've grown up into this wonderful, strong woman. You are kind-hearted, funny, and full of light. You go find the life and the love that you want and deserve."

That's probably the longest speech she'd heard her father give outside of the boardroom. She placed her hand on his arm. "Dad, I'm ready to walk down the aisle."

"You're *sure*?"

"I am positive." Cindy straightened her shoulders. She and her father walked out of the room and she motioned to Bella. The music started playing. She kissed her father's cheek, then determinedly placed one foot in front of the other and walked down to the beginning of the aisle. The aisle with the carefully laid out white chairs, the painstakingly picked out flowers—even if they weren't what her mother wanted—and the precisely tied bows on each chairback. And yet, none of those things mattered to her anymore. How silly to think any of those things were a really big deal, to think they made the perfect wedding.

They stopped at the start of the aisle and she kissed her father. "Daddy, I'm walking in alone."

She took a step up towards George.

Jamie's heart plummeted in his chest and he

clenched his fists as he watched Cindy walk down the aisle. Alone. Where the heck was her father? The music echoed in his brain, taunting him, laughing at him.

Jamie knew he had not much to offer Cindy. Not like the moneyed background she came from. He had only the life at the inn, his friendship… and his love. But, he'd wanted her to make her own decision about George, without interfering. It appeared she'd made up her mind. She was walking down the aisle straight toward George.

He now knew how the term "heart-breaking" came to be, because he was sure his heart was shattering into little pieces in his chest.

Should he interrupt the wedding when the preacher asks "does anyone object to this marriage?" Do they even have that in weddings anymore?

He stared at the scene and couldn't make himself look away. An agonizing emptiness settled over him, almost knocking him to his knees. The sun slipped behind a cloud, plunging the wedding scene into the sweet relief of shade.

Jamie watched in agony, each step of Cindy's taking her further away from him and drowning him in the loneliness that was his future.

Cindy stepped up under the arbor, directly in front of George. The music tapered off. She turned and gave her flowers to Vanessa, and pivoted back to her fiancé.

She looked at him for a just a moment, then reached up and slapped George right across the face.

A gasp went up from the gathered wedding guests.

"Cynthia." Cindy's mother's voice could be heard above the murmurs.

George reached up and grabbed her wrist. "What the heck do you think you're doing?" He glanced quickly at the stunned guests and then back to Cindy. "You're making a spectacle."

He pulled Cindy closer, still with an iron grasp on her arm. She tried to pull her arm free, but he'd have none of it. "Cynthia, pull it together."

Cindy's father strode down the aisle. "George, let go of my daughter."

George looked at Cindy's father in surprise, and dropped Cindy's wrist.

"Cindy, you're embarrassing everyone. What do you think you're doing?" George demanded.

"I'm leaving you at the altar, George. This—*how did you put it to that waitress*—this business deal, that's right. Well, this is one business deal that isn't going to work out."

"You can't do this. You'll be sorry." George took

a step forward. Jamie couldn't stand back any longer and strode down the center aisle. George spun on him as he approached. "This is all your doing, isn't it? You talked her out of it."

"It isn't Jamie's doing. It's mine." Cindy stood toe to toe with George. "Now we can have this conversation here, in front of everyone, or we can step inside."

"You can't just decide not to marry me, you little fool."

"I already did. I won't marry you. You don't love me." Cindy turned away from him. "Oh, and you're a cheater. I won't marry a cheater."

Cindy's father wrapped an arm around her shoulder. "I think it best if you left now, George."

George glared at Cindy's father.

Jamie smiled at Cindy's father, then grinned at George. His heart soared.

"This is going to get messy when we get back to Lexington." George hissed.

"My boy, bring it on." Cindy's father turned his back on George.

George nodded to his groomsmen and they all strode off into the inn.

Cindy's father turned to the guests. "Well, well. This isn't exactly how we had the evening planned, now was it? But I'm so proud of my daughter right now. A man always wants what is best for his daughter. She's proven that she's the strong, independent woman I'd always hoped to raise. Anyone who cares to join us, there is a wonderful dinner inside for all."

Cindy's mother stalked up to the front. "What is going on? Cynthia, have you lost your mind? Henry, what is this nonsense you're spouting? We'll be the laughingstock of Lexington."

"So be it if we are. But I'm betting that most of Lexington knows exactly the type of man George is. I was just too foolish to really see him, to see what he was truly like. He would never have made our daughter happy."

"But all our friends." Mrs. Pearson's voice rose in a panic.

"Our real friends will want the best for our daughter," Henry said firmly.

"I love you, Dad." Cindy reached over and kissed her father's check.

The man chuckled. "You should. It appears I've just paid for the most expensive break-up party ever."

CHAPTER 19

A handful of the wedding guests did stay and enjoy the food at the reception, but most of them left. Cindy asked Susan to make arrangements to send the leftover food to the food pantry and the homeless shelter in the city.

Cindy escaped upstairs, away from her mother and sister and the questioning glances of the wedding guests. She changed out of the wedding dress she never liked, not a bit, and into a simple sundress. She slipped out the side door and headed for Lighthouse Point. No better place to watch the sunset and let this day end and get behind her.

Far behind her.

She strolled along the water's edge and felt at peace for the first time in a very long time. She'd made the right decision, she knew that. Possibly she should have made it sooner, but she'd been unable to see what was right there in front of her. George didn't love her, he wanted a profitable merger. She wanted more. So much more.

She glanced over her shoulder at the sound of someone jogging up behind her.

"Jamie." She stopped and turned toward him.

"Hey, Dream Girl. I just wanted to check on you. I figured you'd head out here."

"You know me so well."

"I do. And, while I'm at it. I thought you were so courageous today. I've never been prouder. You stood up to your George... and your mom and Vanessa. And wow, your dad was impressive. It was quite a day, wasn't it?"

"Dad was amazing, wasn't he? He was so supportive of my decision. He surprised me."

"A day full of surprises..." Jamie's voice drifted off.

They turned and headed toward the lighthouse, silently walking at the edge of the waves. After a while she stopped and tugged on his arm. "Jamie?"

"Hm?"

"It took me a while to figure out that it was not going to be my perfect wedding. Even with the pretty decorations, beautiful views, and at your lovely inn. It would never be perfect if I were marrying George."

"No, I can't say that it would be."

"I was so wrapped up in everything, trying so hard to make it perfect, and trying to please everyone. I was so foolish."

"Sometimes it takes us a while to see what is right in front of us all along."

"You're right. I didn't see George for what he really was, or how I really felt about him."

Jamie reached out and took both of her hands in his strong hands. "I wasn't talking about George, Dream Girl. I was talking about us. You and me."

Cindy took a step back, her thoughts spinning out of control.

He steadied her and continued, "*I* couldn't see what was right there in front of me. This probably isn't the right time, but I've passed up too many chances. I'm not passing this chance to tell you… I… I love you. I've probably been in love with you since we were kids. It's like you're my best friend, the other half of me, the missing puzzle piece."

Jamie squeezed her hands and a shiver skittered through her. "I wanted to tell you this before, earlier this week, but I thought you needed to make your decision about George without me throwing anything else into the mix."

Her heart pounded and her thoughts whirled. "Jamie, I don't know what to say."

"You don't need to say anything. I just wanted you to know how I feel." He smiled at her in the golden light of the sunset, then quietly took her arm as they walked back toward the inn.

Jamie stood in the lobby the next morning watching for signs of Cindy. He hadn't slept a wink last night, he'd just played the evening over and over again in his mind. Maybe he shouldn't have told her how he felt. The timing had been wrong. She'd just blown up her perfect wedding.

But he couldn't *not* tell her. He loved her. He loved her with every bit of his being.

The reporter from Florida Destination Weddings entered the lobby. He'd almost forgotten about that fiasco. He crossed over to where she was checking out at the reception desk.

"I'm really sorry about all this, Jackie. Not exactly the wedding you were planning on covering."

She turned to him and smiled. "This is a beautiful venue for the wedding. I'm still going to do it justice in my write-up. Just so you know, the groom hit on me yesterday—so I'm kind of glad the wedding didn't actually take place. But don't worry, the article will highlight the beauty and organization of the venue, not the hijinks of the groom."

Relief washed through Jamie. "Oh, I'm so glad to hear that. We can use the publicity... without all the dramatics."

"Well, I think the bride did a brave thing. I see so many brides get wrapped up in the whole ordeal of a perfect wedding. They miss out on the important thing. They are starting their life together with their husband."

"Sorry about George hitting on you. I bet you didn't expect that."

"You'd be surprised." Jackie laughed. "I'll send you a copy of the article when it's written."

"Thank you. I really appreciate how well you've handled all of this."

Jackie held out her hand. "Good luck to you and your mother. You have a lovely inn here. I'm planning to come back myself, for a little vacation later this year."

"We'd love to have you."

Jackie turned and walked out of the lobby, and Jamie strode over to the stairs. Should he go up and talk to Cindy again? He ran his fingers through his hair and walked back to the reception desk.

His mother came around the corner from the kitchen. "There you are."

"Morning, Mom."

"I heard you up rustling around most of the night. I thought you might sleep in a bit today."

"Sorry if I kept you awake."

"Anyway, I've been looking for you." His mother reached into the pocket of the apron she was wearing and pulled out an envelope. "Cindy gave me this to give to you."

"When?"

"Early this morning when she left."

"She's gone?"

Jamie's heart sank. She left without giving him a chance to even say goodbye. He reached out for the letter, walked into his office, and closed the door. He slowly sank into his chair and pulled out the note. The heat in the office was stifling, pressing down on him, closing in on him like his life was doing.

He slowly unfolded the note, afraid to read the words, afraid not to.

Jamie,

You are my best friend, and I will always treasure our friendship. You were a big part in helping me realize what a mistake I was making and giving me the strength to stand up to my mother and my sister.

You'd think by this age, I'd be able to make my own choices without worrying about what my mother thinks. It's a lesson I'll need to learn now, to trust my decisions and do what I want, what makes me happy.

Thank you for being honest with me last night and telling me how you feel. Maybe the timing was wrong, but I'm glad you told me the truth.

I need time now. Time to sort things out and figure out what I want, now that I'm finished worrying about pleasing other people or doing what they want me to do.

I hope you can give me that time.

I'll be back, I promise.

Love,

Your Cinderella Dream Girl

Jamie stood and went to look out his window. She was gone without giving him a chance to say goodbye. His day stretched out in front of him in long empty hours. He grasped onto her last line like it was a ring buoy tossed out to him in a storm.

I'll be back, I promise.

CHAPTER 20

R eed pulled his new car onto the bridge to Belle Island. It was a sturdy auto, built like a tank. The safest car he could find. He'd spent weeks driving with an instructor until he felt sure enough to drive on his own. He'd driven daily on short drives and his confidence rose as the summer wore on and fall approached.

He headed to Julie's house to pick her up. He hadn't told her about the car, or the fact he was driving alone again. It was going to be an evening of surprises for Julie. He just hoped she understood the reason for keeping his one last secret. After he talked to her tonight, there would be no more secrets between them.

He pulled up in front of Julie's cottage just as

KAY CORRELL

she was coming out her front door. She stood with her mouth open, then a wide smile covered her face. She raced down the stairs and threw herself into his arms. "You're driving again."

"That I am." He leaned down and kissed her. "I told you I'd conquer my fear. I'd do anything for you."

"I didn't know you'd come this far. I thought... well, I'm happy for you. Did you rent this car?"

"Nope, bought it. Safest car money can buy."

"You *bought* it?"

"Yep, do you like it?"

"I... I'm just overwhelmed by everything." Julie looked dazed.

"Here, let me get your door." Reed walked her around the car and opened her door. She slipped inside, flashing him a delicious look of long tanned legs and bright red shoes.

He drove to his beach house for the quiet night they'd planned. Julie still looked a little dazed as she bustled around the kitchen, finishing up the food for their dinner. It felt so right with Julie here with him. He loved to watch her work in the kitchen. She made most of their dinners here and she was slowly teaching him how to cook. Well, how to help her cook. He'd chop things for her, stir pots, put things in the oven. He still wouldn't claim he was a cook. But each minute spent with her was special.

He'd only made one more trip back to Seattle and one business trip to Chicago. Each time Julie seemed surprised that he came back to her, like she was afraid it would all disappear. He'd give her as long as she needed to become secure in the fact that he was here to stay.

They took their glasses of wine out on the deck while the dinner finished cooking. It was time to tell her the last little fact about himself. He looked over at her with the late evening sun bathing her in a golden light. He was one lucky man.

He swallowed and drew up his courage. "Julie, can we talk for a minute?"

She turned to him with a quick look of fear, like she thought he was going to tell her he was leaving. That look tore at him. He'd do anything to make her feel more secure.

"What is it?" Julie's eyes narrowed the tiniest bit, as if trying not to show her insecurity.

"I don't know how to tell you this, or why I didn't tell you earlier. I know you questioned why I'd go to the expense of renting such a big beach house. You questioned me spending that much. And buying this new car. These were just… small expenditures to me. You see… I… well, I have

money. Quite a bit of it actually. I inherited some…
lots… and I make a really good salary."

"You're rich?" Julie sat up straight in her chair.

"I… well, yes. You could say it that way."

"I'm just finding out now why? You want me to
sign a prenuptial, don't you?" Julie stood up. "Well,
I don't want your money. Your money is yours."

Reed reached out, took her hand, and pulled
her into his lap. "No, it's not that at all. There will
be no prenuptial. What is mine, is yours. I've just
never discussed it with you because, frankly, I was
listed as one of the most eligible bachelors in Seattle
and I always wondered if women wanted to date me
for my money, or because they liked me. Or maybe
they liked me more because I had the money. I
don't know, I was unsure, at least. But with you, I
knew you liked me, for me. You know I felt like I
didn't deserve to be happy again, not since my wife
died, but you've changed all that for me."

He tilted her face up to look at him. "I'd love to
help you out with The Sweet Shoppe. I could help
you expand and do whatever you'd want with the
bakery."

"I don't want your help with the bakery." Julie

looked into Reed's eyes. "I want to do it on my own."

Reed nodded. "I understand. The offer is there if you want it, but I get that you've come so far on your own and want to continue that way."

Julie was still reeling from the knowledge that she was going from a kid in the foster system without a thing to her name, to making it on her own, but barely—to marrying a...*rich* man. It shouldn't make a difference to her, but it did in a way. She was used to being around *normal* people.

"I'll sign a prenuptial agreement. I don't have a problem with that." Julie squeezed his hand.

"No, I'm not going into a marriage claiming mine, mine, mine. I want us to be partners in marriage, in life, in everything. I do want you to know about the money and learn about where it's invested. That's important to me. When my father died, my mother had no clue about anything financial. It was quite a mess. You're okay with that?"

"I guess so." Why did she feel like her world was spinning again, just when she thought she was getting used to the whole marrying Reed thing?

"I don't want us to have any secrets from each other. I didn't plan for this to be a secret, I just never found the right time to tell you."

"So, you're like kinda rich, or like really rich?"

"I'd go with really pretty rich." Reed grinned. "That's why this rental wasn't a problem for me, or the new car. But I don't just throw my money around. I actually have a charitable foundation set up for part of my inheritance. If you'd like to help run it, I'd love your help. You have a good business head on your shoulders."

"I do?"

"You do. Look at all the good business decisions you've made about The Sweet Shoppe. It's really taken off the last few months, along with your catering business."

A charitable foundation. That appealed to her. "What kind of charity work do you do?"

"Mostly charities involving kids."

Julie leaned back against him, feeling his heart beat against her. "I'd like to help with that."

She stared out at the waves rolling in. Her life had gone from one extreme to the other. "It might take me some time to adjust to all this."

"You know I'll give you all the time you need."

"It's just… it's hard for me to truly believe that you won't leave. That you want me. You must have had the pick of any of the fancy socialites in Seattle."

"They weren't what I wanted. I want you."

"It's hard to believe, sometimes. I know you asked about why I was in the foster system. Since we're telling secrets about ourselves tonight. I was in the system because my mother left when I was five years old. Just left. I have no idea where she went or if she's even alive. My father gave me up by the time I was seven, said he couldn't raise me alone. I'm not sure if he was being selfish or maybe he was honestly doing what he thought was best for me. But I had a horrible run of luck with foster families and group homes."

"I had no idea, Julie. I'm sorry. That had to be rough and at such a young age." Reed's deep voice comforted her. "You have no idea where your parents are now?"

"Nope. Haven't tried to find them either. They left me to rot in the foster system. I don't need or want them in my life." It felt so good to say that. To tell someone that her parents had abandoned her. It hurt. It followed her around, an ugly secret hanging over her head. It was part of her past. Her past that she had now shared with Reed. It felt like a load had rolled off her shoulders and he was now sharing her burden.

Reed traced a finger up and down her arm. "I'm glad you told me."

"Well, you started it with the no more secrets decree." Julie smiled a weak smile.

"So we're all good?"

Julie grinned then. "Well, I will be once I get used to the idea of you being filthy rich."

Reed laughed out loud, the rich tones enveloping her in a cocoon of happiness and a feeling of belonging.

CHAPTER 21

It had been a month or so, okay forty-one days —not that Jamie was counting—since Cindy had left. He decided to go drown his sorrows at The Lucky Duck. He yanked open the door and slipped into the cool darkness. A burger, fries, and a cold beer should help. The rattle of dishes, the murmur of conversation, and the spicy aroma of fried food assailed his senses as walked along the bar.

The bartender, Willy, waved at him and gave him the just-a-minute sign. Jamie slipped onto a barstool at the end of the bar, away from the other customers. He just wanted to be alone with his burger and beer.

Willy came over and wiped the counter in front of Jamie. "Long time, no see, buddy."

"Haven't felt much like socializing."

"Heard about the wedding fiasco."

"Pretty sure everyone in town did." Not much was secret here on Belle Island.

"Jamie, you're out and about." His friend Harry slid onto the barstool beside him.

So much for his plan to have a quiet meal. "I gotta eat, you know."

"Or you could have said, 'Great to see you, Harry.' I've been asking you to join me for dinner and drink for weeks." Harry gave him the side eye.

"I know. I know."

"Burger, fries, and beer for both of us, Willy. It's on me tonight." Harry insisted.

"I'm not very good company." Jamie warned his friend.

"Don't I know it? You've been a grouchy old man for weeks now."

Jamie sighed. "You're right. I'm sorry. Let's just kick back and have a nice time."

"Now you're talking." Harry grinned.

Willy looked up and waved at a group of young women coming into the bar. "Be back with your beers in a sec, guys, I'd better go see to those ladies. They look a little lost." Willy winked.

"Lost, huh? I think they look more… ready to party." Harry grinned.

"Gotta give 'em what they want." Willy turned and walked over to the group of laughing women. One of them flirted outrageously with Willy.

Harry nodded over to Willy and the ladies. "He sure knows how to keep the ladies happy."

"Always has. He has an eye for the women. Rarely see him with anyone for very long, though." Jamie wondered how long Willie would joke with the women before bringing their drinks.

A few minutes later Willie slid their beer mugs in front of them. "Ladies, first, don't you know." Willie grinned.

"Of course." Jamie reached for his beer and took a swig.

Harry told him stories of fixing things in the properties he managed, though Jamie only half-listened to the list of broken air conditioners, leaky roofs, and cracked windows. "It's been a hard summer for some of the rentals. Or the people renting have been tough on them. I'm about ready for our slow season. Have a few updates I need to get finished that require an empty property, so I'm waiting until the slower rental season for that. Going to put a new deck on the Jennings property and coordinate new carpeting all throughout the Smith condo."

"That should keep you busy this fall."

"It should." Harry put down his beer and looked directly at Jamie. "How about you. Plans for the fall? Like maybe going up to Kentucky and seeing Cindy?"

"She asked me to give her time. I'm doing just that."

"Maybe she'd like to see you now."

"I'm doing what she asked."

"You're a stubborn one, Jamie McFarlane. Ever think that maybe by now she'd like to hear from you?"

"She knows where I am. She knows how I feel. It's up to Cindy to make the next move."

"If you say so, buddy."

Cindy had avoided going to dinner at her parents' in the two months since the non-wedding. She'd done no socializing at the club and gone to no parties. As she walked into her parents' home, she wasn't sure she'd made the right decision to come tonight.

"There you are, Cynthia." Her mother rose from the sofa and came forward.

"I got tied up at work, I'm sorry." Cindy

glanced at her watch. She wasn't late, just not early like she usually was.

Vanessa sipped on a martini, a look of disdain clearly on her face. "I can't believe you took that job with a hotel chain, for goodness sake. You work such ridiculous hours. You had such a cushy job when you worked for Luxury Interior Designs. Everyone we know uses their services."

Only it hadn't been a great job for her. She'd done a lot of the design work, and the owner took all the credit. She was finished with people taking advantage of her. She'd applied for the job at Hamilton Hotels and shown her portfolio. Delbert Hamilton had hired her immediately to coordinate the interior design of the new hotels he was opening. He was trying to make his own mark on the hotel chain his father had started.

But she didn't bother to explain all that to Vanessa. She just smiled. "I love my job."

Vanessa shot her a doubtful look.

Her father strode into the room, crossed over, and gave her a hug. "I'm glad you decided to come, my dear. I've missed you. How's the job going?"

"It's going great. I'm learning a lot."

"Glad to hear that." Her father reached into the small refrigerator behind the bar and pulled out a beer. "Care to join me?" He held up a bottle.

Cindy grinned. "I'd love to."

Her father popped off the cap and poured a beer into a glass for her.

"Really, Henry. I don't think you should encourage her."

"Encourage her is exactly what we should be doing. Encourage her with her new job, any decisions she makes. We need to be more supportive."

Cindy looked at her father, stunned with his speech.

"But... beer?" Vanessa wrinkled her nose. "Oh, did I tell you? I ran into George at the club. He's dating Gloria Wiltshire."

"Well, good luck to her." Cindy took a drink of her beer. Her father raised his glass to her.

They all walked into the dining room and sat down to the big meal her parents' cook had made. Her mother and Vanessa talked nonstop about people at the club, someone's impending divorce, and Vanessa's newest conquest... Trip Henderson.

"Trip couldn't come tonight. He had a business meeting. He's very busy."

This was Vanessa's third *serious* boyfriend in two months...

"Cynthia, do you want me to check if I can get my hairdresser to fit you in and see if he can do something with your hair if you're going to insist on wearing it down all the time now?" Her mother's face was creased with displeasure.

Her father shot her mother a disapproving glare with a slight shake of his head.

"No, I'm fine with it like it is. Thanks, though." Cindy took another bite of food, wondering how much longer dinner could last. She reached for another roll.

"You're not going to have a second roll are you?" Vanessa's eyes widened.

"Vanessa, you're not to comment on your sister's choices. Not food, not jobs, not… well, anything." Her father admonished her sister.

"But she needs to watch her weight if she wants to start dating good, eligible men again."

The last thing Cindy wanted was to date someone who Vanessa considered an eligible man.

"That's enough, Vanessa. I mean it." Her father set down his glass and glared at Vanessa. "We're not going to play the let's-tell-Cindy-what's-wrong-with-her game anymore. I'm proud of her. She stood up to George and his philandering ways. She went out and got a great job."

Her father turned to her. "I am proud of you. I should tell you that more often. I couldn't be more proud to call you my daughter."

Cindy swallowed the lump in her throat and blinked back tears. "I… ah… thanks, Dad."

"Now, have you done any thinking about that young man back on Belle Island?"

Cindy looked at her father in astonishment. "Jamie?"

"Yes, the MacFarlane fellow."

"The guy that works the front desk at the inn?" Vanessa set down her fork and scowled.

"The guy who *owns* the inn," Cindy corrected.

"But why would Cindy think about him?" Her mother looked truly confused.

"It's clear from looking at him that he cares about Cindy. Anyone can see that. How do you feel about him?"

Cindy wasn't sure she was ever going to get used to this new version of her father. "I… I care about him. I have for a long time. He… he's the best friend I've ever had."

"And what are you going to do about that?" Her father raised an eyebrow.

"Jamie, quit slamming the drawers." Susan looked at her son.

"I can't find the darn paperwork with the estimates on painting the front of the inn."

"And slamming drawers helps?"

"It does." He slammed another drawer.

"I'm sorry you're hurting."

Jamie looked up at her and sighed. "She hasn't called. Not once. I haven't spoken with her in three months and two days."

"She said she needed time, son."

"How much time? What if she never comes back?"

"She'll come back."

"You don't know that for sure." He jerked the missing file from the stack of papers on his desk with a flourish. The pages cascaded to the floor. He swore, then quickly looked up. "Sorry, Mom."

"I was going to go meet up with Tally and Julie, but maybe it would be better if I stayed."

"No, I'm fine. I'm sorry. I am. I don't mean to take it out on you. You go on."

Susan crossed over and put her hand on Jamie's shoulder. "Okay, I'll be back soon, though. Then maybe you should take a break."

"Maybe." Jamie leaned down and started scooping up papers.

"I'll be at The Sweet Shoppe. Back soon."

"Have a good time."

Susan left the inn and quickly walked the distance to The Sweet Shoppe. The September morning was still hot and sunny and she relished the bit of freedom she had from work in the slower fall season, even as she regretted the loss of customers at the inn, the ebb and flow of island business.

She pushed inside and waved a hand in greeting to Tally and Julie. They were already seated at a table by the window with a carafe of coffee and plate of baked goodies on the table. She had no idea how Julie stayed so thin surrounded by all the delectable things she baked.

"Sorry I'm late. Jamie was in some mood when I left. I'm worried about him."

"He still hasn't heard from Cindy?" Tally scooted out a chair for Susan.

"No, and it's driving him crazy."

"Maybe he should go see her." Julie set down her cup of coffee.

"She asked for time, and he's giving it to her. Jamie's heart is breaking a little bit more each day she stays away, though. I can see it."

"I think she'll be back when she's ready." Tally's voice was filled with conviction. "She needs some time to figure things out. It's clear she cares about Jamie."

"I hope you're right."

"Tally's always right about love, haven't you heard?" Julie grinned. "I listened to her and see where it got me."

"How is Reed?"

"He's great. All settled into his big old house. You guys saw how big it is, didn't you? Though, it does have a killer view." Julie picked up her coffee and set it right back down. "I... well, we had a talk the other night. There are some things I didn't know about Reed."

"More secrets?" Tally's forehead wrinkled.

"Well, it's more like details he didn't tell me. Like he's... rich. I mean really, really rich."

"No kidding. Doesn't act like it."

"So, it seems he inherited a bunch of family money along with making some big old salary at his job. He regularly has a driver and a housekeeper. He showed me pictures of his home and it's... *large*. Like estate large."

"And you had no idea?" Susan asked.

"He said that women were often interested in him for his money. He's known around Seattle as the rich eligible bachelor. He liked knowing that I fell for him, the man, not him the man with money."

"How do you feel about all this? Did he tell you

this because he wants a prenuptial or something?" Susan knew all about prenuptial pitfalls.

"No, actually he specifically said we weren't going to have one. What is his, is mine. I'm just not used to thinking about having money like that."

"You're still going to keep The Sweet Shoppe, aren't you?" Tally leaned back in her chair.

"Of course."

"Well, then I don't see what the big deal is. He's a good man. I guess a *rich*, good man." Tally smiled. "He obviously loves you."

"I think it will just take me time to get used to the idea of having money. He offered to upgrade the kitchen here, or move me to a larger space, but I don't want his help. This shop is something I've made on my own. I want to keep it that way."

"He understood that?" Susan asked.

"I think so. I hope so. He did ask if he could have the van seat recovered where the spring is poking out of the rip in the vinyl now that he's driving. He says he wants to help with deliveries when he has time."

Susan laughed. "I'd let him do that."

"I might." Julie grinned.

Susan looked over at her friend, getting ready to marry into money. She was once in that exact position. Well, not exactly. She and Russell hadn't been madly in love, and Russell hadn't wanted to share any of his money.

Okay, nothing like it at all.

"So when you were talking to him, did you discuss a wedding date?" Susan was all ready to host the wedding at the inn if that's what Julie wanted.

"We talked about it, but I didn't commit to anything yet. It's all so… well, it's all so much. I can't believe it's happening to me and I keep thinking the other shoe is going to fall."

"You deserve the happiness you're getting." Tally reached over and covered Julie's hand. "You just need to believe that you're worth it and reach out and take all the happiness that Reed is offering."

CHAPTER 22

"Jamie."

He turned at the sound of his name. Harry crossed the deck of the inn.

"Your mother told me I'd probably find you here."

"Did she tell you that she basically threw me out of the inn? She'd been over with Julie and Tally and came back and just... tossed me out."

"Might have mentioned that. Might have asked me to talk to you." Harry grinned. "So I guess Cindy really got under your skin, huh?"

"You could say that. It feels like all those years ago when she left and never came back."

"But she *did* come back."

"To marry that jerk, George."

"But she was smart enough to call it off." Harry leaned against the deck railing.

"Then she disappeared *again*. It's been three months now. Three months. Well, three months and two days."

"So, you love her, right?"

Jamie looked at his friend. "I do. I admit I fell hard for her when she was back here. I'd forgotten how easy she is to be with. We connected again, and I hope I get a chance with her. You know, if she ever comes back."

"I bet she will after she has some time to process everything. I mean she was all the way up to the altar with that George guy. She probably just needs time."

"I'm giving her time, it's just not easy. I… miss her. Miss talking to her."

"Buck up, old man. You're driving your mother crazy."

"I know I am. I'm driving myself crazy. Arguing with myself about calling her or not. Heck the other day I almost jumped in my car to drive to Kentucky to see her. Not that I even know if she's back home in Kentucky. I have no idea how she's doing."

"Well, listen to your mom and go take a long walk and clear your head."

"I probably should before my mother strangles me. I know I've been hard to live with."

"You have been. We all want the old Jamie back." Harry pushed off the railing. "I'll catch up with you later."

"Thanks, Harry. I swear I'll get it together soon."

Harry raised a hand in a brief wave as he crossed the deck and slipped inside the inn. Jamie turned and trudged down the steps to the beach.

Jamie headed to Lighthouse Point. His mother was right, he'd been in a foul mood for days. Well, pretty much since Cindy had left. He'd been willing to give her space, he just hadn't known how hard it would actually be. Every single day he'd wanted to pick up his phone and call her. Every single day he had to talk himself out of it. He knew she needed time. She'd asked for it. He needed to respect her wishes, even if it was slowly killing him.

He should shake himself out of his mood, though, because it wasn't fair to his mother, or Dorothy, or anyone around him.

But he missed her with every breath he drew.

Cindy stood on the front porch of Belle Island Inn,

gathering her courage to go inside and find Jamie. He was probably mad at her for not contacting him in over three months. She just hadn't known what to say to him and needed time to sort things out. But it was way past time to talk to him. She pushed through the door and headed inside.

Susan looked up from the reception desk and a warm smile quickly spread across her face. "Welcome back."

"Hi, Susan."

"Well, I know someone who will sure be happy to see you."

"I have a new job with Hamilton Hotels and we are opening a hotel in Sarasota. I'm doing the interior design for the hotel. I love it. So challenging and rewarding. I just got to Sarasota last night and drove straight over to Belle Island today after checking on a few things for the hotel. Is Jamie here?" There was this slight doubt nagging her that Jamie had changed his mind, that she'd waited too long.

"I just sent him out for a walk. He's been a bit *difficult* since you left."

"I'm sorry."

"No, don't be. He said you needed time and wanted to give it to you."

"Jamie always knows what I need and gives it to me."

"You can wait here for him, or try to find him."

"I bet he headed to Lighthouse Point if he was upset."

"Good guess." Susan grinned.

Cindy's heartbeat quickened. "I'll find him."

Susan nodded as Cindy turned and hurried out the door. Within minutes she was quickly walking along the familiar water's edge, headed toward Lighthouse Point. She spotted him as soon as she made it around the bend. He was standing with a hand shielding his eyes from the glare of the sun as he watched a blue heron fly methodically over the waves. She quickened her pace, her heart pounding and her emotions doing flip flops with every step she took.

He turned and saw her as she got closer. A grin spread across his face and he started walking towards her. She ran into his waiting arms and he swung her around with a laugh. "You're back, Dream Girl."

"I am back."

"Man, I missed you." Jamie murmured the words against her ear as he held her close. His heart beat in rhythm with hers, in perfect sync, which didn't surprise her. They'd always been in perfect sync. It had just taken her a while to find her way back to him.

"I missed you, too. So much. Things kept happening and I wanted to talk to you, but you weren't there."

"No, I was here, waiting for you to come back to me."

"Thank you for giving me some time." She pulled back and looked up into his eyes. "I'm back now, if you still feel the same way. I love you, Jamie. I think I have for my whole life."

Jamie looked down at her. "I love you, too. I can't imagine ever being with anyone else."

"I feel the exact same way. I not only love you, you're my best friend, the one I want to share everything with."

Jamie pulled back from her and she frowned. "What's the matter?"

He dropped to one knee in front of her. "I don't have a ring yet, but I'll fix that immediately. I love you, will you marry me?"

"Oh, Jamie. Yes. Yes, I'll marry you." She dropped to the sand beside him. "Let's get married. Really soon."

"Let's do just that, Dream Girl." With that,

Jamie pulled her close and kissed her slowly and gently, pressing against her lips. It took her breath away and she was sure she saw fireworks and heard angels singing. This, *this* is what it was like to be in love.

CHAPTER 23

Cindy couldn't ask for a more perfect October day for her wedding. The sun was shining, the temperature was warm, not hot. She and Jamie invited just a few people. Her parents and Vanessa came, but her father held a tight rein on any comments her mother or sister might make. Josephine, Paul, and Bella came, along with Harry. Tally, Julie, and Susan completed the wedding guests. A simple wedding with every detail exactly how Cindy wanted it.

Susan stopped by the room where Cindy was getting ready. "I just wanted to tell you how glad I am that you're marrying Jamie. I wanted to welcome you to the family."

"Oh, Susan. That means a lot to me." Cindy hugged her almost-mother-in-law.

"You make Jamie very happy, which is all I ever wanted for him." Susan's face lit up and her eyes sparkled with joy.

"He makes me happy, too."

Susan squeezed Cindy's hand. "You look lovely."

"Thank you." Cindy spun around in her simple, white dress. "I love this dress."

"It's the perfect dress for you." Susan smiled. "I'll see you outside."

As Susan left, her father came into the room.

"You ready to do this?" Her father held out his hand for her.

"I am so ready, Dad." She was. Her heart was full of love and she was so sure of her decision.

"I think you've made a good choice, marrying Jamie. He's a fine young man."

Cindy took one last look in the mirror. Her hair hung in curls around her shoulders. She wore simple white flats. She took a deep breath, placed her hand on her father's arm, walked outside onto the beach, and down the aisle to Jamie. Her heart soared as she took each step closer to him. Jamie reached out and took her hand when she got to him.

Jamie turned to her father. "Don't worry, sir. I'll take good care of her."

"I'm sure you will, son."

Jamie squeezed her hand, leaned close, and whispered, "You look beautiful."

They said their vows and the minister pronounced them husband and wife. Suddenly she was Mrs. Jamie McFarlane. Everything fell into perfect place in that one moment. Together they would navigate through life, sharing their dreams.

Jamie kissed her slowly and thoroughly and everyone burst into applause. She took his arm and walked across the sand, back down the aisle as husband and wife.

At the end of the aisle Jamie whispered, "Are you happy, Dream Girl?"

"I am. I did get my wish after all. My wish at Lighthouse Point. I got my perfect wedding." With that, Cindy stood up on tiptoe and kissed her husband, the perfect man to share the rest of her life.

THANK YOU for reading my story. I hope you enjoyed it. Sign up for my newsletter to be updated with information on new releases, promotions, and give-aways. The signup is at my website, kaycorrell.com.

Reviews help other readers find new books. I always appreciate when my readers take time to leave an honest review.

I love to hear from my readers. Feel free to contact me at authorcontact@kaycorrell.com

~

COMFORT CROSSING ~ THE SERIES

The Shop on Main - Book One

The Memory Box - Book Two

The Christmas Cottage - A Holiday Novella (Book 2.5)

The Letter - Book Three

The Christmas Scarf - A Holiday Novella (Book 3.5)

The Magnolia Cafe - Book Four

The Unexpected Wedding - Book Five

The Wedding in the Grove (crossover short story
between series - Josephine and Paul from The Letter.)

LIGHTHOUSE POINT ~ THE SERIES

Wish Upon a Shell - Book One

Wedding on the Beach - Book Two

Love at the Lighthouse - Book Three

Cottage near the Point - Book Four

Return to the Island - Book Five

INDIGO BAY ~ a multi-author series of sweet romance

Sweet Sunrise - Book Three

Sweet Holiday Memories - A short holiday story

Sweet Starlight - Book Nine

ABOUT THE AUTHOR

Kay writes sweet, heartwarming stories that are a cross between women's fiction and contemporary romance. She is known for her charming small towns, quirky townsfolk, and enduring strong friendships between the women in her books.

Kay lives in the Midwest of the U.S. and can often be found out and about with her camera, taking a myriad of photographs which she likes to incorporate into her book covers. When not lost in her writing or photography, she can be found spending time with her ever-supportive husband, knitting, working in her garden, or playing with her puppies—two cavaliers and one naughty but adorable Australian shepherd. Kay and her husband also love to travel. When it comes to vacation time, she is torn between a nice trip to the beach or the mountains—but the mountains only get considered in the summer—she swears she's allergic to snow.

Learn more about Kay and her books at kaycorrell.com

While you're there, sign up for her newsletter to hear about new releases, sales, and giveaways.

WHERE TO FIND ME:
kaycorrell.com
authorcontact@kaycorrell.com

Join my Facebook Reader Group. We have lots of fun and you'll hear about sales and new releases first!
https://www.facebook.com/groups/KayCorrell/